A CHRISTMAS TO CHERISH

JOSIE RIVIERA

This book is dedicated to all my wonderful readers who have supported me every inch of the way.
THANK YOU!

CHAPTER 1

*E*mmanuelle Sumter surveyed the picturesque town of Cherish, South Carolina, brightly lit in crimson and green holiday decor. The town looked as if it had emerged from a Christmas card. Glittering frost framed bare tree branches, and local artists were setting up their canvases for an art walk. The coldness in the air was soundless and serene, comforting in its own way.

She exited the Cherish Central train station, zippered her cobalt-blue puffer coat to her chin, and stepped onto the curb.

Who believed an actual, breathing town could resemble a holiday snow globe?

Evidently, her friend Dorothy did, considering her enthusiasm whenever she described her idyllic South Carolina town.

Emmanuelle stood on the curb and shoved her hands in her pockets. A cold December gust slapped her cheeks, sharp streams of frigid air. She swept a wisp of hair from her cheek and searched for Nicholas, Dorothy's older brother. He was supposed to pick her up. People were shouting greetings, kissing, cooing over babies. A teeming mass of humanity.

But no Nicholas.

A taxi's horn spiked. Emmanuelle jumped, an involuntary nervous reaction.

Take a deep breath. Relax. Dorothy had assured her Cherish was a safe haven, a harbor in a storm.

Repeating her mantra, Emmanuelle hailed the black-bearded taxi driver parked at the curb. She still didn't see any sign of Nicholas, so she'd take the cab.

She handed the driver her suitcase, then slid into the backseat and gave the address of Dorothy's music store, Musically Yours.

They passed charming shops decorated in glittering lights, and a sign advertising a historic home tour. A few minutes later, the driver pointed at the Musically Yours lighted outdoor sign and idled at the corner of Myrtle and Magnolia Streets.

"The store's two hoots and a holler away, ma'am." He hoisted her suitcase from the trunk and set it on the side-walk. "We've reached your destination."

Destination. Was this where her journey ended after a year filled with pain and abuse? Did hope and encouragement wait for her in this little town?

A new life. With perseverance, she could start fresh.

"Thanks." She climbed from the taxi, paid the driver and grabbed her suitcase.

Daylight faded as dusk crept in, and she tipped her head to take in Evergreen Street. Family-owned businesses had switched on their storefront lights, transforming the town into a fairy-tale sparkle of miniature white lights. The tanta-lizing scent of honey roasted almonds wafted through the air. Boughs of fragrant holly tied with red velvet bows hung cheerily from tall solitary lampposts. Bright-faced children skipped by, lifting their faces skyward to catch a sprinkling of snow. Their conscientious parents followed close behind.

"Emmanuelle! You arrived right on time!" Dorothy flung open the door of the music store and pressed a welcoming kiss to Emmanuelle's cheek. Dorothy's brown hair was swept up in a French braid, her creamy complexion glowing with an enthusiasm Emmanuelle didn't recall from their days working as struggling musicians in New York.

Dorothy had lived there before moving back to Cherish, her hometown, and marrying her high school crush, Ryan Edwards. He had been an opera star in the making and had given up his touring career to settle in Cherish. They were newlyweds. They were in love.

Love. The beginning was always so alluring. It was the end Emmanuelle feared.

Dorothy regarded the departing taxi. "Apparently Nicholas didn't pick you up?"

"I didn't see him so I took a cab."

Emmanuelle turned from Dorothy and admired Musically Yours' frosty window display, bedecked in an infinite array of treble clef signs. A pine wreath, embellished in antique ornaments—tiny pianos, violins, and harps—adorned the front door.

"It's wonderful," she said. "You've worked so hard to set this up."

"Thanks. Ryan and I are still learning the business, and we're inspired by anything musical."

Emmanuelle smiled, but then shivered. "It's colder here than I expected. At least the blizzard that threatened to shut down New York never came."

"The storm hit after you left," Dorothy replied. "You escaped the worst of it."

Did she? She couldn't answer at first, finally whispering, "Hopefully."

Dorothy raised a delicate eyebrow, but Emmanuelle didn't elaborate. Sure, she'd escaped the snowstorm. An escape from George, her ex, was yet to be determined.

Please God, be with me now in my dark season, when I'm so out of place. The world around me is glowing with the promise of Christmas and I feel dark and empty inside.

She leaned forward to admire two animated polar bears sitting amidst the treble clef signs in the shop's window. Beneath a starry sky, the bears tapped drums to the tune of "Jingle Bells."

"Very clever." She couldn't help a grin. "Thanks for the invite to Cherish."

"We're thrilled you agreed to join us for Christmas." Dorothy grabbed her hands for a reassuring squeeze. She was so pleasant and gracious, Emmanuelle thought. So jovial.

On the other hand, Emmanuelle felt the opposite. All she had become in twenty-five years—a dependable, straightforward woman as well as an esteemed harpist—she'd lost in six months to George.

She'd once been like Dorothy, resilient, independent and a woman of God.

Her ex had taken it all away.

Deep in her coat pocket, her fingers worried an angel ornament she'd purchased at the New York airport. For her, the ornament symbolized the sacred Christmas season, its optimism, dreams, and promise.

She hadn't taken it out of her pocket yet.

"You've been difficult to reach these past few months." Dorothy studiously appraised Emmanuelle. "You hardly ever answered your phone."

"I've been busy with concert engagements." Emmanuelle forced her features to remain blank. "You know, musician stuff." It was a lie, and with the lie came heaviness, a wide band of disapproval. Where had her sense of decency gone?

She tightened her paisley scarf around her neck. Although the violent purple and yellow bruises had faded, she still felt self-conscious.

Dorothy guided her into the music store. "My brother will blame his forgetfulness on his new job, or that gigantic puppy he adopted at the animal shelter. You'd think he'd know better at thirty years old."

"He's a good guy," Emmanuelle said. "Nicholas and I Skyped every night for months when you were in rehab."

"Thanks to you both, I'm better." Dorothy smiled. "And most important, thanks to God."

Once, Emmanuelle would have readily agreed. God was her salvation, her refuge. Now she didn't know how to answer because her faith had wavered.

Truly I tell you, if you have faith as small as a mustard seed, you can say to this mountain, "Move from here to there," and it will move. The verse from Matthew 17:20 came to her mind, a reminder of her strength. All she had to do was reach for it, if she was brave enough.

Inside the store, Dorothy ran a finger along one of the shelves, grinning when she was assured it was dust free. "Ryan and I purchased a cottage-style bungalow four blocks from here and there's an extra bedroom."

"This is your first Christmas as a married couple." Emmanuelle set her suitcase out of the way of a passing customer. "Please celebrate the holiday without me in the middle."

"I insist you stay with us."

"For an entire month?" Emmanuelle shook her head. "Insist all you want. I booked a room at the Cherish Hills Inn. You raved about the inn's accommodations being top-quality when you returned to Cherish for your brother's wedding last year."

"The wedding that didn't happen." Ruefully, Dorothy

sighed. "Nicholas is still healing from the embarrassment and heartbreak."

The ending stages of love. Dreams shattered.

Without warning, the front door burst open. Instinctively, Emmanuelle held up a hand, shielding herself from view.

A heavy-set woman, her hair helmeted in a tight gray bun, ambled inside. She called out a jovial hello to Dorothy.

"Be with you in a minute, Mrs. McManus." Dorothy gave a flap of her hands, and then turned back to Emmanuelle. "Sorry. What were we discussing?"

Emmanuelle blew out a breath. This uneasiness, this fear of being followed, had to stop.

Still shaken, she kept her focus on a Mozart statue topped with a red plush Santa hat sitting on the counter.

"We were discussing the wedding that didn't happen," she replied. "Whenever Nicholas and I talked when you were in rehab, he always reminded me we should place our trust in God."

"Sadly, people change, beliefs change." Worry replaced Dorothy's earlier smile. "Hard knocks can shake the faith of the most devout. I pray he'll go to church again because he's faltered since the breakup."

Suggesting Emmanuelle put her suitcase behind the front counter, Dorothy led her past a display table. As Dorothy paused to rearrange two pairs of oboe earrings so they lined up side by side, she said, "God had other plans for him and for me. I believe things work out for the best."

Emmanuelle frowned and nodded, aborting both actions.

For Dorothy, perhaps. For Ryan. For anyone in this idyllic snow globe town. But not for me. And apparently not for Nicholas.

Her cell phone buzzed. She retrieved it from her tote bag and scanned the screen. *Unknown caller.* Her heart stopped. A telemarketer? A wrong number?

"Who is it?"

Looking up, she saw Dorothy was studying her with keen interest.

"No one." Fumbling, Emmanuelle tucked the phone back into her faux leather tote. "You're right. People change for many reasons." And she'd changed most of all. She'd been a competent, successful woman. Now a chill crept up her spine when a door opened into a harmless music store.

"Are you okay?" Dorothy asked.

"I'm fine, just tired from traveling." Emmanuelle's eyes welled with tears, and she averted her gaze. She'd applied makeup, the first time in months, attempting to conceal her sleep deprivation. The endless worrying and crying had taken a toll.

"We're organizing a concert in the town square the weekend before Christmas," Dorothy was saying. "I meant to ask you to bring your harp—"

"My harp weighs nearly eighty pounds." She picked up a pair of piano earrings and fingered the tiny keyboard. "It's in New York."

Broken. She wouldn't reveal how George had destroyed her harp in one of his lightning-fast rages. The memory caused a block of ice to form in her stomach, a block that she knew would be slow to thaw. She hated the thought of her beloved instrument, splintered into pieces, lying on a New York curb under a pile of snow.

Better the harp than you splintered into pieces.

But his shouted insults and rough slaps had been her fault. She'd provoked him.

No, no, no. Her inner voice took on a sharp edge. That was the old Emmanuelle talking. The new Emmanuelle knew she wasn't a dishtowel to be thrown around on a whim. In hindsight, she should have known George was abusive. The warning signs were there.

7

She blew out a breath. She'd resolved to find peace and comfort in this holiday … in this town … somewhere … and find her footing again.

"Enough about me." She set down the earrings and dismissed herself with a flutter of her fingers. "Where's Ryan?"

"He's rehearsing in nearby Stanley Valley today and will arrive this evening. He'll be singing 'O Holy Night' for a Christmas Cantata service. He gives so freely of his talent." Dorothy's smile was as radiant as a Merry Christmas bouquet. "He's featured throughout the Carolinas in many guest appearances. Plus, the Atlanta opera house asked him to perform the role of Zoroastro in Handel's opera, *Orlando.* I'm incredibly proud of him."

"You should be." Dorothy's smile was contagious, and Emmanuelle managed a warm grin. "He's famous and extremely talented."

"And you? Any upcoming concerts?"

"None." She answered in a firm tone that she expected would discourage her friend from probing. Judging by the way Dorothy's eyebrows drew together, she'd succeeded.

Fortunately, an acoustic guitar arrangement of "Lo, How a Rose Is Blooming" piped in the background, the ideal holiday music to smooth a lull in the conversation.

"I'm sure you're keen to check in." Dorothy broke the silence. "I'll deal with these last few customers, close the store, and give you a lift. Unless you'd rather walk the three blocks to the inn?"

"No, no. I'll wait for you."

She'd never walk alone again. Not in New York, not in Cherish. Not anywhere, because she'd never feel safe again.

Dorothy gestured toward the front of the store. "If you care to browse, the Christmas music section is on your left. There's a lovely harp arrangement of *The Nutcracker.*"

"Thanks. Your store is a music-lover's dream."

Intrigued, Emmanuelle stepped past a buyer laden with music bookmarks and made her way to the sheet music. She thumbed through endless arrangements of Christmas solos, wondering what madness had brought her to this town. She didn't belong here among all this gaiety. Her sadness was a burden refusing to go away.

Disheartened, she stared, trancelike, at the display window. A whimsical model train circled the polar bears, and the sight was enchanting.

Beyond, past the cheery town, past the exuberant children and the enormous Christmas tree illuminating the town square, a darkened sky had followed dusk.

CHAPTER 2

*A*s he entered his apartment, Nicholas Thompson pulled off his deputy badge and set it on a table in the foyer. Except for one traffic violation, a minor fender bender and endless meetings, the day had been relatively calm for a newbie deputy.

He looked forward to relaxing in front of the TV with a good cup of coffee and a chocolate-glazed doughnut. Ever since he'd become a deputy, he'd acquired a taste for both.

All fifty pounds of his six-month-old golden retriever greeted him with an energetic stretch. He'd purchased the dog from an animal shelter in Stanley, two weeks to the day after his fiancée, Alice, had broken up with him. The dog surveyed Nicholas with expectant black eyes and a fiercely wagging tail.

"No, Molly Belle, I'm not taking you for a—"

The dog ran in circles around him and barked.

Nicholas groaned. He'd no sooner walked in and he was forced to turn around and walk out again. "All right, take a tater and wait a sec." He weaved around a mountain of laundry and strode to his bedroom. His bed was unmade, an old sweat-shirt tossed over a side chair. He removed the gun from his holster and locked it in his bedroom closet's safe. Then he loosened his tie and changed out of uniform—white shirt and khaki pants—dragging on jeans, a long-sleeved T-shirt, and work boots. Pausing, he ran a critical survey of his apartment, particularly the coffee table piled with remote controls and junk mail and old catalogues. The large sofa begged for a skilled reupholster, and his sister, Dorothy, had admonished him countless times to hang curtains on his bare windows.

He darted a glance at the motorcycle calendar propped on a shelf. Today was December first, and Christmas was less than a month away. At the very least, the season merited a Christmas tree in the corner and a wreath on his apartment door.

Nope. Not this year.

Despite Molly Belle lightening his days, Nicholas didn't have the heart for celebrations and feasts. What other man in the state of South Carolina had experienced the humiliation of his fiancée leaving him on their wedding day? And by text, no less. Not even in person.

The dog's impertinent barking prompted him to grab the leash, button his navy pea coat and open the front door. With an eager yelp, Molly Belle ran ahead, down his short flight of stairs and onto the sidewalk.

"Slower, girl." The dog, as usual, didn't obey and tugged harder on the leash. Nicholas made a mental note to sign her up for obedience classes.

His cell phone buzzed. He hoped it wasn't a call to drive back to the police station. Relieved to see Dorothy's caller ID, he clicked on.

"Nicholas, are you through with work?" she asked.

"Yes, I just got in." He restrained the dog from sniffing

every blade of grass in a neighbor's garden. "I'm taking Molly Belle for a walk."

"Emmanuelle arrived an hour ago. Did you forget?"

He sighed and slapped a hand to his forehead. He forgot a lot of things lately. "I got sidetracked by last-minute meetings at the police station. Please tell her I'm sorry."

"You can tell her yourself. We're at the Cherish Hills Inn and she's unpacking. Meet us here, then join us at Frank's Pizzeria for a slice. It's your favorite restaurant."

His first response was *no* before he thought better of it. He should extend a polite apology, considering he'd forgotten to pick up the woman. He'd swing by and make his amends and then leave.

As he and Molly Belle neared the inn, it was all he could do not to reverse direction and head back to his apartment.

He could work. He could take care of his spirited dog. But he didn't relish small talk with a woman, especially a woman he'd grown close to during their many phone conversations. What would he say to her after all these months?

"Oh, by the way, Emmanuelle, do you remember me talking nonstop about Alice, my fiancée? She left me the day of our wedding."

Molly Belle ignored his command to walk slower, nearly choking on the leash as she lunged forward.

CHAPTER 3

*B*attling for control of the leash, Nicholas strode into the Cherish Hills Inn's lobby. Briefly, he admired the boxwood wreath hanging on the wooden door, the lighted village scene on a round cherry tabletop in the foyer. He greeted the white-haired innkeeper, Tom Canning, with an apologetic shrug and lifted the dog's leash.

Tom scowled. Crevices grooved the sides of his mouth. "No animals."

"Just this once—for someone you've known your entire life?" Nicholas asked. "For a man who upholds the law in our town?"

Tom sighed, unbending a bit, and peered at Nicholas above the cheaters perched on the bridge of his nose. "Go ahead, deputy." He rewarded Nicholas with a brief nod, but raised his index finger to issue a one-minute warning.

"Thanks." Nicholas strode across the wide plank floors to the parlor where a fire blazed in the stacked rock fireplace, so large an ox could stand upright inside it. On the center of the mantel sat a handsomely carved Nativity set in burnished wood. Artistically arranged seasonal fruit—oranges and apples and pears—were loaded high in a wide pewter bowl on a side table.

He directed his gaze toward Dorothy, who stood near the fireplace, and that was the last thing he remembered.

The undeniably beautiful woman who stood beside Dorothy, clad in a white lace sweater dress, resembled a dainty, sweet confection. Her complexion was pink, her dark lashes slightly lowered, her lips plush and generous. A puffy blue jacket was slung over her shoulders, and she held a tote bag close to her side.

His mind reeled with memories.

Emmanuelle Sumter. They'd Skyped many times, so he'd known she was attractive, but in person she was positively breathtaking. Silky blonde hair rioted around her face in impossibly tight curls, and her huge blue eyes acknowledged a tentative welcome.

"I assume you remember me." He fumbled with Molly Belle's leash as the dog sniffed the rug incessantly. "You look … different in person." *Better*, he amended to himself. *She looked better. More than better.* He extended his free hand. "Please accept my apologies for forgetting you."

"Apology accepted." She placed her small hand in his large one. "How could I forget our nightly conversations? You guided Dorothy through a challenging season in her life."

Emmanuelle's features were so petite, her fingers so fragile. "And you were the friend she counted on." He tightened his grip and vigorously shook her hand.

"You were the person who prayed with her every day." She pulled away, politely, decisively. "You encouraged her."

"Hold on you two, I'm right here!" Dorothy laughingly stepped between them. "Are you competing in a compliment contest I'm not aware of?"

Emmanuelle's dimples winked in a slight smile. "Your brother's the winner."

"Please don't boost his ego, or he'll expect you to treat for pizza." Dorothy chuckled. "Frank's Pizza is within walking distance. They advertise the best pizza in town."

"Because they're the only pizzeria in town." Nicholas helped Emmanuelle on with her coat, then swung Molly Belle's leash up and down. "Unfortunately they don't allow animals and I won't be able to go."

Molly Belle responded with a defiant stare and Emmanuelle leaned down to pet her. "Aww, your dog is so friendly." Soon, the dog was lying on the rug legs up, outstretched in doggy ecstasy while Emmanuelle crouched to rub her stomach.

"You said you'd just gotten home from work," Dorothy said as she encouraged Emmanuelle and the dog to stand, then steered the threesome to the doorway. "Have you eaten dinner, Nicholas?"

"I'll whip up something." He couldn't imagine what although there was a slight possibility a frozen pizza sat in his freezer behind a carton of peanut butter ice cream.

Molly Belle had different ideas, having decided Emmanuelle was her new best friend. With a wiggle of glee, she changed direction and hurled straight into her.

Emmanuelle fell back and Nicholas let go of the leash to stop her fall. Freed from her leash, the dog shot in another direction and knocked over a crystal vase filled with red roses. The vase shattered on the floor.

Tom, eye-glass cheaters in hand, tore into the parlor. His face colored to a beet-red as he tapped his watch. "Your one-minute dog visit was up five minutes ago, Nicholas."

"Sorry. We were just leaving." Nicholas righted Emmanuelle as Dorothy picked up the roses, then he dashed forward to retrieve the leash.

"Shoo, all of you!" Tom said. "I'll clean up the mess."

The women followed Nicholas. They exited to a whip of

icy wind that blew Emmanuelle's curls around her face. Nicholas lifted his hand, an automatic response to protect her from another gust. She flinched, tightened the pink paisley scarf around her neck, and moved a step away.

He tossed an inquiring glance toward her. She ignored him.

As if by mutual agreement to cover up Emmanuelle's skittish behavior, Dorothy began talking about every holiday event scheduled in three counties between Christmas and New Year's.

"Frank's boasts an outdoor enclosed eating area," Dorothy continued, talking in a loud voice to drown out the quiet. She stopped briefly to commend the florist shop's front window decorated in scarlet-red poinsettias and twine wreaths. "I'm sure Frank's will allow Molly Belle inside, Nicholas. She's leashed and we'll take an out-of-the-way table."

Before Nicholas could comment, Dorothy's cell phone pinged. She grabbed it from her tote bag, read the text, then extended an unapologetic grin. "Ryan returned early from Stanley. A few weeks ago, he bought a cookbook called *Southern Charms* at a fundraiser for encouraging women empowerment, and he's been learning to cook gourmet. He's preparing a romantic dinner of rosemary chicken and pasta salad and he wants me to come home now. He has a surprise for me."

"I applaud your husband for buying a cookbook and supporting a beneficial cause." Despite his words, Nicholas sent his sister an exasperated glance. "So, you invited me to join you for dinner and now you're leaving?"

If she was trying to fix him up with Emmanuelle, he refused to go along with it. From what Dorothy had revealed, Emmanuelle had accepted his sister's offer to visit Cherish for the holidays primarily to get away from New York. The result of breaking up with a man. It was always because of a man, he thought, reflecting on his cheating fiancée and her new boyfriend.

He wanted to extend a sympathetic ear, for surely Emmanuelle wanted to talk at length about the break-up, although he wasn't in the proper frame of mind to attend to anyone's problems other than his own.

Yes, he'd gotten along well with her. They had talked nightly for months because of their shared interest in Dorothy's welfare, plus their unshakeable faith in God. But his life was different now. His faith teetered. If he had to define it, he'd say his faith was lukewarm.

He tuned back in when he heard Emmanuelle say, "Don't disappoint Ryan." She put her hand on Dorothy's arm, then flashed a look at Nicholas. "I'll double back and finish unpacking if you don't mind walking me."

This was his out. A polite response and he'd be sitting in his recliner watching television within fifteen minutes flat. Instead, he found himself saying, "We're almost at the restaurant so we might as well enjoy dinner."

Besides pizza, the restaurant had good coffee.

"Perfect! You two go on without me. I'm sure there's a lot to catch up on since you haven't talked in a year." Dorothy tucked her brown hair under the black wool cap she produced from her handbag. With a satisfied wave, she swung in the opposite direction.

"This way." Nicholas touched Emmanuelle's arm. She sidestepped him and ran a hand over the zipper of her jacket. Although she appeared to be an elegant and poised woman, she was as edgy as a newborn fawn.

Perhaps there was nothing left to discuss? Dorothy, their commonality, no longer required their help, and he obviously wasn't interesting enough for pretty and popular Emmanuelle. The thought left him maintaining a chilly and reserved silence as they walked toward the restaurant.

His gaze landed on two tow-headed toddlers running ahead of them. They pointed to the fairyland of Christmas lights in the town square and the sight made Nicholas smile. He loved children, although now he'd never have any. He'd never subject his heart to another battering. He'd successfully barricaded himself behind a solid, protective shell.

Lonely? Sometimes.

Safe? Definitely.

He headed Emmanuelle and Molly Belle toward the next block.

Molly Belle had a mind of her own, though, wanting nothing more than to loll on the sidewalk and hug the ground. He encouraged the dog with an assurance of a treat, and Emmanuelle added a "C'mon girl."

When they resumed walking, he asked, "Are you still the principal harpist for ... I forgot the name of the symphony. It was in a town somewhere outside New York."

"No, I'm not playing the harp anymore. It's gone." Stillness reigned for several beats after her self-deprecating laugh. He recognized the defeat in her shining blue eyes, and sympathy flickered in his hardened heart.

"What about you?" The audible stress in her tone made him hesitate. "I remember you were studying for an important exam."

"The police academy. I passed and I'm a deputy."

Her eyes widened. "A—a deputy ..." She blanched and missed a step.

"And here I thought congratulations were in order," he half joked.

"Yes, of course." She clutched her tote bag and kept her head down. "Umm, congratulations, Deputy Thompson."

Something had happened to her in New York. Something bad, although he couldn't offer any support because he was empty. The woman whom he'd thought had loved him had left him flat. He'd been a blind fool while she'd deceived him for months, but he'd learned a painful lesson and he'd learned it well. Relationships with women were well off his radar, especially when a woman clearly had a hang-up about men.

Bachelorhood was serene. Naught to fear, because nothing—no hearts, no feeling, no plans—would be broken. Besides, a dog was excellent company.

Despite himself, his gaze lingered on Emmanuelle's profile, her slim figure she kept well-hidden beneath her winter jacket and high boots.

Molly Belle barked a little too enthusiastically, prompting Emmanuelle to jump when a black lab trotted past.

"She's high-spirited," Nicholas offered as an explanation.

"Who's in control here?" she asked him. "I used to work around dogs. They were a big part of my life." She patted Molly Belle's head, then smiled when the dog put a wet nose in her hand.

"I'm considering dog obedience classes. Do you think it's a good idea?"

Emmanuelle opened her mouth, closed it again, grinned. "Yes, it's an excellent idea. In the meantime, begin with simple commands like *sit* and *wait*. Can you do that?"

"Certainly. I'm the master."

An irreverent chuckle burst from her lips and he fought the insane impulse to kiss her.

He knew her through those lengthy phone conversations, and every night he'd looked forward to their discussions about God, and their everyday lives, and their pasts. Their comfortable hour-long chats had become easy and familiar. If he hadn't been engaged to his fiancée at the time, he might have admitted the attraction he'd felt for Emmanuelle.

This stiffness between them was foreign. She had frequently sought his advice, the comfort of his faith coinciding with her hard-won beliefs. She'd been orphaned when she was in her teens, but she had persevered, studied hard, and become a virtuoso harpist.

They walked the last block to the restaurant at a quick pace. Her knee-length dress glided along her legs and her suede boots fit high above her knee. Nicholas kept stealing glances at her. The self-sufficient woman he'd known had evaporated. She'd become breakable, her voice soft, her movements hesitant.

They walked up the steps to the pizzeria's entrance, and he reached around to open the door.

"I'm ordering Frank's deluxe-meat lovers special," he said. "Are you the salad type?"

"Salad? Salad is for vegetarians." She walked past him into the restaurant, her expression amused. "I'm the barbecue and corn fritters type."

CHAPTER 4

$\mathcal{T}$he next day was Saturday, and Nicholas worked a half day. The morning had started with an arrest for drunk driving and ended in the police station with multiple copies of blank forms to fill out. He loved his job, but he could do without the written procedures and minute details.

When he returned home at noon, he changed out of his uniform and into jeans and a shirt, a white pullover hoodie, and running shoes. He dashed off a reminder note to price affordable curtains over the weekend, then leashed Molly Belle for a quick jog.

Ryan's surprise for Dorothy the previous night had been tickets to a tuba Christmas concert in Stanley, and Dorothy had given Nicholas the not-so-subtle hint that Emmanuelle would be spending the day alone. Despite telling himself a firm *no*, he found himself veering toward the Cherish Hills Inn.

Their dinner at the pizzeria had ended abruptly when Emmanuelle had pleaded tiredness soon after he began telling her about his job as deputy sheriff. He'd started off by regaling her with amusing tales of some of the absurd arrests he'd made. One had been for drunk and disorderly conduct when a spectator ran onto the field of a high school football game declaring he was the sixth offensive lineman. On another occasion, he'd walked an eighteen-year-old home to face his parents after a keg party had gotten out of control, only to have the boy get sick on their front lawn.

As he talked, Emmanuelle's shoulders had tightened and her hand quivered as she'd pushed the barbecue around her plate. Her fear was tangible, stretching across the red-check-ered tablecloth, and the pizza set neatly in the center of the table.

He got the hint and stopped talking about his profession altogether, carrying on instead a reasonably normal conver-sation, albeit one-sided, observing the average winter temperature in South Carolina and New York.

The inn neared, and he closed the distance to the porch steps in five long strides.

He leaned forward to catch his breath and wipe his brow on the sleeve of his hoodie. Wide-slatted rocking chairs were assembled on the expansive front porch and evergreen garland and holly berries were strung across each window.

Although he normally would simply walk into the inn, after the mishap the day before, he thought it best if he knocked first.

Pushing his cheaters down his nose, Tom Canning peered through the entry's side glass, glowered, and flung open the door. "No dogs allowed inside, Deputy Thompson." He tried to sound polite, but there was no mistaking that he was issuing an order. "No exceptions."

"I'm sorry about yesterday, Mr. Canning, and I'll be happy to pay for any damages."

"Good. I'll write up a bill for you."

"No hurry. I mean, please do." Nicholas kept a sneakered

foot in the door as the innkeeper attempted to shut him out. "Will you let Emmanuelle know I'm here?"

Tom took off his cheaters and polished them. "Is she expecting you?"

"Probably not."

"Hi Nicholas." Emmanuelle appeared at the bottom of the curved staircase, looking bewitchingly beautiful. Her blonde hair was piled high at the crown, her ever-present pink scarf around her neck, her puffy blue jacket all zippered.

"I guess she was expecting you." With a conspiratorial half grin toward Nicholas, the owner ushered them outside, then slammed the door, leaving Emmanuelle and Nicholas standing on the porch with Molly Belle.

Annoyed, Nicholas fixed his gaze on the door. "I thought everyone loved animals. Apparently, Tom doesn't like dogs."

"His reasons are excellent." She didn't withhold her chuckle. "That vase of roses spilled water across his rug and cost him thirty minutes of clean-up, not to mention the cost of the vase and flowers."

"I offered to pay for the damages." Nicholas inspected her trim, shapely form. Today, black jeans and high boots accentuated her long legs. A green sweater peeked from beneath her winter jacket. "Were you ... expecting me?"

The color on her cheekbones rose to a flattering blush against her creamy complexion. The afternoon sun gilded her blonde hair to streaks of platinum, and he favored her with an unabashed smile. She was stunning.

She stretched on a pair of pink knit gloves that matched her scarf. "Dorothy mentioned you might stop by."

"Several local booths in the town square are selling Christmas items. Are you up for some last-minute shopping?" He was prepared for her to refuse. However, he didn't expect the wariness on her face, the absolutely motionless air between them.

"I have no reason to shop. I'm not buying any Christmas gifts this year." She focused a pained stare on the mixed greenery placed around the white rocking chairs.

An unexpected fury flowed through his veins at whoever had hurt her. When? Where?

"Surely there's something you'd like." He grinned, an attempt to disarm her. "The locals sell handmade jewelry and artwork and leather goods. And I have it on excellent authority that one of my friends, who owns a restaurant called The Grill Room, set up early this morning and is smoking South Carolina barbecue as we speak."

She considered her watch. "It's a little late for lunch."

"It's just shy of two o'clock. We'll call it an early dinner." He hooked his thumbs in the back pockets of his jeans and felt the leash go slack. In an instant, his dog had raced off the porch in a mad chase after a squirrel.

"Molly Belle!"

What happened next occurred in slow motion.

The dog ran into the road. Brakes squealed. A sickening thud.

"No!" Unmindful of traffic, Nicholas dashed for his dog, seeing only Molly Belle's limp body lying helpless in the middle of the road. Blood seeped from her stomach, matting her glossy golden fur. He sank down, right there with his dog, and did something he hadn't done since he was a child.

He cried.

CHAPTER 5

*E*mmanuelle sat in the passenger seat of the innkeeper's lime-green Volkswagen and held the dog in her lap while Nicholas drove. She controlled her voice as she rubbed Molly Belle gently behind her ears. She'd secured a makeshift muzzle using the dog's leash, assuring Nicholas even Molly Belle, a sweet dog, could lash out when she was in pain.

"Looks like a surface wound," she said. Carefully, she lifted the dog's lip, murmuring about capillary refill time. When Nicholas didn't seem to hear her, she added, "Fortunately, the driver stopped in time."

Everything had happened in a blur. Visibly distraught, the driver had burst from his car in a frenzy and groped for the words to apologize. Tom Canning rushed out and offered Nicholas his car, and then dashed to the inn. He was back almost instantly with sterile gauze and a yellow crocheted blanket an instant later. A bystander stopped traffic, which allowed Nicholas and Tom to use the blanket as a sling and carry the dog to the car. Emmanuelle placed gauze over the dog's stomach and applied pressure, murmuring relief when the blood didn't soak through.

Nicholas drove quickly and silently to Cherish Animal Hospital. She took in his granite profile, his short blond hair shoved back from his forehead. He hunched behind the wheel stuffed into a car not made to fit his six-foot frame.

"She doesn't appear to be in shock." She kept her voice quiet and upbeat.

His dog might not be in shock, but Nicholas was. He had taken immediate action, though, and had phoned the animal hospital to tell them they were on their way.

"You don't know that," he finally responded.

"Yes, I do. I've been around plenty of sick dogs."

When they arrived at the hospital, Nicholas parked near the entrance. Once more using the blanket as a sling, they carried the dog past a red-haired receptionist who announced that her name was Scarlett Evans.

Dr. Judson Troutman, the veterinarian, waited for them in the examining room. Nicholas had mentioned to Emmanuelle that Dr. Troutman had been widowed two years earlier.

Slim, serious, and sandy-haired, the vet was casually dressed in khaki pants, a button-down shirt, and a white lab coat. After brief introductions, he checked Molly Belle's lungs with his stethoscope and confirmed Emmanuelle's evaluation. The dog wasn't in shock.

"My father was a veterinarian," Emmanuelle said. Reverently, she ran a hand along the stethoscope after the vet had laid it to one side.

"You learned well, Emmanuelle." His deep-brown eyes were kind, his demeanor innately gentle. He angled toward Nicholas. "I'm going to give Molly Belle all the time she needs, Deputy Thompson. After her fluids are stabilized and the diagnostics run, I'll give you an update. For now, there's nothing else to do except sit and wait."

Scarlett ushered them into the reception area. A nervous-looking woman in her fifties cradling a quivering black dachshund bobbed a brief hello.

Emmanuelle slid onto a thinly padded chair and nudged aside a half-finished cup of coffee set on a corner table. She rubbed her arms and then dropped her head into her open hands. Now that her adrenaline had settled, she felt chilled and kept her jacket and scarf over her shoulders.

Nicholas paced the hallway for several minutes before coming to sit beside her. "I don't know why I wasn't paying attention and didn't hold onto her leash tighter. If only I had …" He stared down at his hands.

She scanned his clenched fists, the skin bunching at his eyes. "Molly Belle is blessed with the ability to love life. You're the most important part and not to blame. She's always on a leash and you do all you can to keep her safe."

Her quiet reassurances seemed to help, for he sat straighter.

"Still, I was lax. Will she ever forgive me?"

"Of course."

She didn't know where to put her hands, so she rested them on her lap.

Scarlett ushered the nervous woman cradling the dachshund down the long hallway. A door banged shut.

"The accident should never have taken place." Nicholas scrubbed his fingers over his face. "I can't make sense of it. Lately, I can't make sense of anything that's happened to me."

"Everything in our lives is a result of God's favor."

"Favor? What favor? My cycle of believing has been broken."

"So was mine. Whenever I think about the person I became these past few months, it makes me sad."

"What happened, Emmanuelle?" He studied her expression. "When we last spoke on the phone you were so upbeat."

She chewed her bottom lip. "A lot happens in a year. Don't ask me about the in-between because I'm not ready to talk about it." Mentally reliving George's abuse, a heavy despair settled in her gut. Whenever he'd banged her body into a wall, he screamed that they belonged together, and he was trying to teach her who was the master. No one had ever hit her before. She'd come from a kind and loving home.

"You were only meant for me, Emmanuelle."

The psychological, and then physical, abuse was always worse after George drank. The sharp smell of whiskey on his breath predicted the flashes of unpredictable anger sure to follow. A familiar sweat of panic slid down her neck. On a jerk, she swung her gaze from Nicholas and locked the terrifying remembrances in a safe compartment in her mind.

"Emmanuelle?"

She faltered, found her axis and drew a fortifying breath. "Dorothy stopped by the inn this morning."

"Why?"

"To talk. And she reminded me I shouldn't rebuke myself for past circumstances. She encouraged me to keep my attention on God and not dwell on myself."

"How can a memory upset you if it already happened?"

"Now there's a question I ask myself. Memories can only upset you if they have your attention. The key is to focus on what really matters." Despite her brave declaration, she couldn't meet his probing stare. Instead, she eyed the white-lighted snowman, accented with sheer purple ribbon, hanging on a far wall.

After breakfasting with Dorothy in the inn's sunny conservatory, Emmanuelle had confessed the beatings she'd suffered while tears had streamed down her cheeks. With every frightening scene she confided, heavy chains had been lifted from her heart.

Dorothy was kindhearted and understanding, a true friend, her intentions always in the right place.

Emmanuelle's rapport with Nicholas was different. He had commended her on her talent and independence, complimenting her on countless occasions. What would his opinion be if he learned she had been foolish enough to allow a man to control her?

She released a sigh and hid her face in her hands. She carried a shame she couldn't describe, not even to herself.

"Care to discuss what happened to you, Emmanuelle?" Nicholas repeated. "You can trust me."

He stared at her. She stared at the snowman.

She could hear a cell phone ringing in the hallway. She could smell the cold, stale coffee on the corner table.

Yes, she trusted Nicholas, even as she feared his admiration would change to disapproval once he understood her situation.

Why hadn't she left George sooner? She'd asked herself the same question more times than she could count.

"Because, Emmanuelle, you were meant only for me."

She shuddered, recalling his bloodshot gray eyes, as he was liquored up more often than not. When had he changed? He'd been so charming at the outset of their relationship, wooing her with lavish dinners and dark chocolate truffles and evenings at the theater.

"Emmanuelle?"

Despite her resolve to start a new life, she pressed her lips tight and didn't acknowledge him.

"You know," Nicholas went on, "I once was a person of great faith." He inclined his head and spoke softly. "This dejection I've felt ever since Alice—"

Emmanuelle's words came quick with no apology. "Your sister said, "'If you despair, you will live in despair.'"

"Dorothy is admirable and Ryan has taken her lead. Together their faith is anchored in God. I want to trust in the Lord again, I really do." He lifted his hand and cupped her chin, raising her face to his, forcing her to meet his gaze.

She didn't flinch, knowing that he needed a fresh start, needed her full attention.

"Begin by reaching out in prayer." She took his hand, holding it as he bowed his head and whispered praises to God. Silently, she joined him.

Scarlett strolled over, stacking used coffee cups and folding morning newspapers. "Do you two want anything? There's coffee in the vending machine."

Nicholas looked up at her. "Is it any good?"

"No. It's instant, and cold, and shuts off sometimes. Often, actually." She grinned. "Anyway, I brought in extra junk food from home. You know, candy and cupcakes, bottles of soda. Want anything?"

Emmanuelle smiled. "We're fine, thanks."

"My motto is to embrace life and indulge yourself."

Scarlett's full-figured form, Emmanuelle noticed, was pleasing and curvaceous. She was empathetic and sunny, a person who saw the bright side, even on a bleak afternoon. Upbeat, she finished cleaning up the waiting room and retreated to her desk.

As afternoon slipped into evening, Dr. Troutman emerged from the hallway. He drew up a chair to sit across from them. "Delightful news, Deputy Thompson. Surgery isn't necessary. There's no internal bleeding, organ damage, or broken limbs."

"She's going to be all right?" The guarded hope in Nicholas's voice prompted Emmanuelle to place her hand on his arm.

"Molly Belle will be fine." The vet came to his feet. "You can take her home tonight. Find a comfortable spot and get her settled with some heating pads. Given time, she'll heal with no scars."

"Thank you, doctor."

"Clean the wound and apply an antibiotic cream. I gave her an injection for her discomfort." Dr. Troutman rooted in his lab coat for a pad and pen. "I'm prescribing an anti-inflammatory and I recommend not leaving her alone for extended periods of time."

Nicholas's face paled. "For how long? A week?"

"Recovery time varies. She's a young bouncy dog, and I predict she'll be fit in a few weeks or less. Incidentally, she might be a mixed breed. Although she's mostly a golden, I'm thinking there's a bit of yellow lab mixed in." He scribbled the prescription and handed it to Nicholas. "I'll ask Scarlett to schedule Molly Belle for a check-up next Saturday."

"Are you sure I can properly care for her at home in the meantime?" Nicholas hesitated before starting for Scarlett's desk. "If it's safer, please keep her overnight for observation."

"Nothing to observe. You and your girlfriend are quite capable," Dr. Troutman said. "She knows her animals."

"I'm not Nicholas's girlfriend," Emmanuelle clarified, quick to get to her feet. "I learned a tremendous amount when I helped my father. We lived in Remsen, a little town outside of New York. For years, I visited his office every day after school."

From the corner of her eye, she saw Nicholas's thick eyebrows raise as he busied himself with paying the bill.

"How far outside of New York is your father's office?" the vet inquired.

The memories flickered, faded, a million miles away. Once, she'd felt safe and happy, living like other people. How easy it had been when she was a child.

"He died ten years ago when I was sixteen." She spoke carefully, not letting her sense of loss, her free and easy childhood, creep into her voice. "He was a highly regarded veterinarian in our little town. Cherish reminds me of Remsen. Without Remsen's snow."

"I've never been to Remsen," Scarlett chirped. "I bet it's pretty there."

Dr. Troutman gave Scarlett an indulgent smile, then turned back to Emmanuelle. "A small town's down-to-earth values and its focus on what matters most in life ... Well, there's not much that can beat that."

"You're absolutely right." Emmanuelle extended her hand. "Thank you."

Over at the reception desk, Nicholas handed Scarlett his credit card, then peered over his shoulder at Emmanuelle. "All those hours we spent on the phone and you never mentioned your animal expertise."

She shrugged. "There were more serious topics to discuss."

Saying he would get Molly Belle, the vet walked down the hallway. He and Nicholas transported a muzzled Molly Belle to the rear seat of the Volkswagen using a large dog crate.

On the drive to Nicholas's apartment, Emmanuelle pondered what to do. Torn between the belief that helping for a week wouldn't matter because she had no other plans, and the fact she'd be immersed in his personal surroundings, she considered how to word her offer before she spoke.

He needed help, especially when he reported to work on Monday. Yet, he hadn't asked for any. A proud, stubborn man, Dorothy had once described her brother when she'd become frustrated at his inability to talk about his hurt after his marriage plans fell apart.

"Once Molly Belle is situated tonight," Emmanuelle began, "I'll stay with her while you fill her prescription."

"I appreciate that."

Guarded, yet so polite.

"Once Monday rolls in, I'll watch her while you're on duty, deputy."

"Wouldn't you rather kill time checking out the Christmas markets and visiting Dorothy and Ryan?"

"I'd rather kill time being of some use."

"All day nursing a sick dog isn't a vacation." His expression indicated his willingness to accept her offer, although he kept his tone carefully noncommittal.

"Who said my visit is about a vacation? Christmas is the season for giving."

What else could she say that was a reasonable justification for offering to help? She simply *wanted* to because Nicholas and Molly Belle had become important to her, but she certainly couldn't say that. "I have experience tending to sick animals."

"I'll pay you." He offered a quick, grateful smile.

"Do you cook?"

"Do frozen pizzas count?"

"You're describing the extent of my cooking skills as well." She grinned. "Fortunately, Ryan is learning gourmet cooking so I'll throw out some hints. Or better yet, I'll borrow his *Southern Charms* cookbook."

CHAPTER 6

*W*ith Molly Belle settled on a blanket near the recliner in the living room, Nicholas went off to get her prescription. Emmanuelle applied a heating pad to the dog's belly, where it seemed she had the most pain. When she was assured the dog rested comfortably, she removed the heating pad and waited for Nicholas to come back with the prescription.

Dr. Troutman's injection had made Molly Belle drowsy. Her brownish-black nose pressed upon the blanket, and her sides rose and fell as she dropped into in a deep, sound sleep.

In the solitude of the quiet room, Emmanuelle set to work tidying the coffee table. She boxed up old magazines and catalogues that lay scattered in a mismatched pile beside five remote controls. Why did a man need so many remotes for one television set?

When Nicholas returned, he hung his hoodie by the door and crossed the room. Crouching, he stared at his sleeping dog.

"She's asleep and not in pain," Emmanuelle assured him. "See? Her tail is twitching. She's probably dreaming about chasing purple pigeons or flopping in the grass at the Cherish Hills Inn. When she wakes up, we'll give her the medicine."

Nicholas nodded. "And I have bad news and good news." He rolled to his feet and handed her a white paper bag. "The bad news is the kiosks were closing. The good news is I managed to plead our upsetting afternoon to my friend from The Grill Room. He was smoking a beef brisket and added coleslaw. I figured you were hungry. I also snagged a couple cups of coffee and two honey-glazed donuts."

She gave an appreciative sniff. "My mouth is watering."

He went to the kitchen and pulled a water from the fridge. "What do you want to drink?"

She followed him and put the kettle on the stove to boil. "Hot tea. Thanks."

He folded his shirtsleeves to his elbows and draped a dishtowel over his shoulder. "My place is a mess, although I used to be fairly neat."

"I think I have enough tidying here to keep me occupied."

"Yeah, for at least a year." He grinned, then grew solemn. "Since my failed engagement to a woman who—"

"You didn't fail." She reached for a thick mug in the cupboard. "Your fiancée did."

They dished out the smoked barbecue brisket and coleslaw and brought stoneware, napkins, and utensils into the living room. She placed the stoneware on the coffee table, set her napkin on her lap, and took a neat bite of brisket. Chewing, she nodded toward Molly Belle. "After she sleeps, she may be sore. Follow the directions on the prescription."

"You'll come ... tomorrow?"

She reached for her tea. "I texted Dorothy to let her know what happened. She and Ryan are still in Stanley. She'll stop in tomorrow to see you and the dog."

"And you?"

"I'll be here on Monday morning, as long as you don't mind leaving the dog by herself to come get me."

"The weatherman calls for a pleasant week. Sunny and highs in the fifties. If you'd prefer to walk—"

"I never walk alone anymore, but will walk with Molly Belle." She gulped her tea and set the mug on the coffee table, and then her napkin alongside it. "However, can you drive me to the inn? It's getting late and I'm sure the innkeeper will be worried. Besides, you have his vehicle."

"I phoned Tom, and he knows Molly Belle is fine. He assured me he isn't leaving the inn tonight." He rested his hand lightly on hers. "Please stay a while longer. You haven't finished your brisket, and I could use the company."

Hesitantly, she replaced her napkin in her lap.

Nicholas relished his meal as if he hadn't eaten in a week although she nibbled and pecked at hers. After they finished, he lifted his water for a last pull while she cupped her mug and stared out the narrow window. A splash of light streaked across the black velvet sky.

"You realize we're in full view of your neighbors." She grinned at him over her mug. "One of them is cruising into their driveway."

"Dorothy has reminded me on a weekly basis about buying curtains."

Still holding her mug, she wandered to the window and considered the quiet night covering the sleepy town. The room stilled to a comfortable silence.

"I've been waiting for a beautiful woman to come along who can help me choose the right ones," he said. "Fortunately, I've known her all along."

She pivoted, catching his wicked grin and look of interest as his gaze focused on her face. Her pulse leapt in a disconcerting combination of anticipation and panic.

"Emmanuelle." His voice grew quiet. "I can hardly kiss you when you're standing on the other side of the room."

"Nicholas, we hardly know each other."

"A year ago, we talked regularly. Our bond was strong. Let's be honest. We both know it still is."

She walked to the couch and set down her mug. He set down his water. Their gazes held, the quiet punctuated by the dog's light snores.

Her thoughts scattered. She rearranged them into a semblance of reason. "A year ago we had a common purpose —ensuring your sister made a full recovery."

"Are things so different?" Gently, his fingers curved around her nape, soothing, stroking. "I'll help you make a full recovery from whatever you're struggling with." He bent his head slowly, and his lips met hers with sweet tenderness.

For a moment, she went rigid.

"I'm attracted to you, Emmanuelle," he murmured. "Always have been. I'm here for you."

Her body reacted in a dizzying sensation of emotions she couldn't explain. She didn't want to respond to him. Or perhaps she did because her reaction felt so natural. Trusting a man, feeling safe and cared for in his arms ... She'd thought those feelings happened to other people.

Tentatively, she reached her arms around his neck and returned the kiss.

His mouth deepened as he fit her response to his own. He kissed her fully, insistently, boundlessly, creating a knot of pure awareness in her stomach. The longer his mouth pressed to hers, the more vibrant the sensations became. It was as if a new person had taken the place of the broken Emmanuelle. The new Emmanuelle was sincere and receptive, the former hesitant and uneasy, avoiding any connection with a man.

A sharp woof broke them apart.

Molly Belle lifted her head and regarded them. Before Nicholas could get to her, she laid her head down and went to sleep.

Emmanuelle's lips twitched. "Her injection is wearing off."

He settled on the couch and watched Emmanuelle, his gaze heated. "Shall we continue? We left off at—"

"Your dog may wake up again."

"I'll take my chances." His arms slipped around her, and she reveled in the pleasure of his hard mouth pressed on hers. She kissed him back while his warm hands shifted protectively around her.

Ages later, he lifted his head and cradled her face. Affection smoldered in his hazel eyes. "You came into my life at exactly the right time."

Molly Belle stirred, twitched, woofed to no one in particular, then plunked her nose back on the blanket.

He chuckled. "I think I have a love-hate relationship with that dog." With a sigh, he lowered his hands from Emmanuelle's face. He forked a last bite of coleslaw, leaned against the couch, and stretched out his legs. "Stay a while longer. Please. I'll be sure you make it back to the inn before midnight, Cinderella."

Across the inches of the couch separating them, she met his stare. His striking features were full of hope, almost boyish.

He was an honest man. Genuine and steadfast, his every movement capable, yet easy-going.

"All right, but only because you said 'please,' Prince Charming."

He reached out and gathered her to him. "Remember the night we watched television together when we were Skyping?"

"How did you ever persuade me to stream a documentary

about the Hubble telescope when I had a concert to prepare for the next day?"

He threw back his head and laughed. So good-natured, so familiar. "You should thank me because you learned several new outer-space terms. And all the planets—Mercury, Venus, Earth—"

She laid her hand on his arm. "I'm a musician, not an astronaut."

"Where is your harp, by the way? In New York?"

She kept her features blank and tried to make her voice impassive. "My harp is gone."

His expression was thoughtful as he obviously sensed her bleak mood. A beat passed.

"One of my favorite memories," he said, keeping her in his arms, "is the night you played the harp for me. 'Danny Boy.' Remember? I'd had an argument with Alice, and you said music would soothe me, so you lit candles and darkened your apartment. You had told me your harp was accented in twenty-three karat gold. I remember it shimmered in the candlelight each time you plucked a string. Truly, Emmanuelle, you looked like an angel, and it gave me goose-bumps." He traced her cheekbone with his forefinger.

"You sang while I played," Emmanuelle said. She'd clung to the memory of those shared times, although she'd known he was engaged and never pressed him for anything other than friendship.

Not long afterward, Dorothy had gotten out of rehab for opiate addiction, and Emmanuelle had met George, the wealthy hotel magnate.

And George had taken away her harp. Her pride. Her life.

CHAPTER 7

*N*icholas felt like he danced through the following week, and he wasn't a man who'd ever managed more than a two-step.

Molly Belle improved every day. She had reclaimed her sleeping spot at the foot of his bed, ate regularly, and reveled in her short daily walks with Emmanuelle. She'd even taught the dog to "sit" by holding a treat near the dog's nose. Once Molly Belle was sitting, she'd repeat the command, give the dog the treat, and shower her with affection and praise. She'd repeated the same sequence throughout each day, then demonstrated Molly Belle's progress for Nicholas each evening.

She'd taken Molly Belle to a shop a few doors down from his place and selected a fresh pine wreath, simple and unadorned, that she'd hung on his front door. On another occasion, she purchased curtains in a dazzling shade of lipstick-red and hung them on his bare living room windows. The effect was homey, warm, and Christmassy.

She'd also experimented with cooking new dishes. Thanks to Ryan's *Southern Charms* cookbook, Nicholas never knew quite what to expect for dinner. He only knew an exotic, savory meal waited for him when he got home.

In the evenings, he and Emmanuelle dined in his cozy kitchen, on a wooden table tucked beside a snowy window, polishing off spaghetti carbonara and thick slices of buttery bread accompanied by oven-fried pickles.

"Surprise me," he'd tell her each morning after she'd arrived.

And she did.

He enjoyed her companionship, her considerate nature, the way her dimples flashed whenever she was amused. He hadn't found a word to put to his feelings, especially since he hadn't wanted to become romantically involved with a woman after his breakup with Alice.

With Emmanuelle, though, the word *love* came to mind.

On the last day of the work week, Nicholas issued his customary thank you to her as soon as he strode through his apartment door. Molly Belle wriggled with delight, bounded to his side and greeted him with a continuous train of wet doggy kisses.

He scrubbed a hand along the dog's ears.

Emmanuelle was seated on the couch, intent on studying a page from Ryan's cookbook.

"I've been thinking about dinner all day," he said. He'd been thinking about her too, although he didn't mention that part. For a celebratory end-of-the-week supper, Emmanuelle had declared she was experimenting with a different fix on a traditional Christmas recipe—roasted turkey and sweet potatoes garnished with a fancy topping Nicholas had forgotten the name of.

He slid his gun from his holster, took off his badge. "How was your day?"

"Busy. Despite her size, Molly Belle thinks she's a lap dog." Emmanuelle kept her head down, busy flipping pages.

"And Dorothy and Ryan invited us for Christmas dinner so I tried a new dessert recipe tonight too."

He breathed in a lungful of smoky air just as the smoke alarm went off. "Is something burning?"

"Oh, no!" The cookbook fell from her lap as she jumped to her feet. "I forgot to set the timer."

They sprinted toward the kitchen. The dog whined and raced in the opposite direction, scratching at the door to be let out.

"I was testing a fruitcake recipe," Emmanuelle said as he opened a kitchen window to let out the smoke, and then turned off the alarm.

Not a dreaded fruitcake. Since Nicholas was fairly intelligent, he kept the comment to himself as he retrieved the burnt cake from the oven and set it on the counter. He commiserated with Emmanuelle, sighed, and tried to look regretful. He wanted to joke about the fruitcake making a good doorstop and wisely changed his mind.

"The cake can't be salvaged, so I'll phone for pizza delivery," he said. "Sound good?"

"If you stopped to look around, you'd see I cooked a twelve-pound turkey and sweet potatoes. Is pizza your fix for whatever comes your way?"

"There's no such thing as bad pizza. So …yes." He lifted the foil off the potatoes and pointed accusingly. "What's this white stuff on top?"

"Goat cheese and scallions."

"Sounds awful …" He caught her scowl. … "fancy." He congratulated himself for thinking so quickly on his feet. "Sounds awful fancy. Do you think I'll like it?"

"Fifty-fifty."

He suppressed a chuckle. She looked positively intoxicating, even with her heart-shaped mouth twisted into a grimace as she beheld the burnt cake.

He left the kitchen to check on the dog, who'd resumed her place at the foot of his bed.

When he returned to the kitchen, he drew off the hairband she'd used to secure her hair when she cooked, brought her closer, and embraced her for a lengthy kiss. "We're beginning to sound as if we're a couple, and I like the sound of it."

She drew an unsteady breath and dropped her gaze, but not before he noticed the warmth kindling in her vivid blue eyes, the flush of heat tinting her creamy complexion a soft pink.

"We can't be a couple."

"Why not?"

She kept her gaze rooted on his bare wood floor. "Because I won't be a burden to you." She placed her arm between them, an effective wedge.

He'd half expected her reaction.

Anything to do with Molly Belle's care prompted an easy conversation. So did the latest recipe in the cookbook. Or classical music, especially her favorite composer, Beethoven. She responded to his kisses, molding herself to him. But any talk of a serious relationship put her off-balance.

He drew her to the couch and took a seat beside her. In an attempt to lighten the mood, he teasingly bumped her shoulder with his. "Tomorrow is Molly Belle's vet appointment. I'm hoping you'll go with me."

"Absolutely."

He smiled, relieved. He'd come to rely on her for emotional support.

"Afterward," he went on, "I'd like to buy a Christmas tree. My apartment is begging for a dose of holiday cheer, so are you up for a stop at a tree farm outside of town? In the past I've cut my own tree." He gestured to the dog. "Because she's still recovering, we'll buy a precut tree."

"Perfect." Her smile was luminous and lit his small apartment with merriment.

The attraction sizzled between them. Soon, he thought, when she was ready, she'd tell him her trepidation, and he'd assure her she was safe. Mutually, they'd dismiss her worries. She was in Cherish where life was secure. He'd keep her out of harm's way—whether real or imagined.

Trying to tamp down his eagerness, he reached into his shirt pocket and withdrew a small box wrapped in gold paper with a red satin ribbon. "Thank you, Emmanuelle, for everything you've done for me this week. On my lunch hour today, I stopped at Musically Yours and bought you something." He held the box out to her.

Lightly, she touched her hand to his. "Nicholas, you didn't have to buy me anything. I wanted to take care of Molly Belle."

His senses buzzed, alive to the brush of her fingertips, the thickened skin where calluses had formed. Once she had told him she was proud of those calluses, a badge for practicing long hours to pursue her dream of becoming a professional harpist.

And she had.

He'd taken her suggestion to give God his attention and had begun praying every night. Lately, he'd lifted a plea that she'd make Cherish her permanent home.

She could build a life here. *They* could build a future together.

He slipped an arm around her waist, delighting in her nearness, staring at her for a long moment. "I wanted to buy you a gift. It was my pleasure."

"Nicholas …" She ran a hand through her unruly blonde curls. Her chin trembled. Although they'd known each other for over a year, she grew unexpectedly shy.

"Please open it." He stilled her hand and kissed her

temple. He was giving her what he could. He wanted to give her so much more.

Nodding brightly, she rapidly undid the paper and unlatched a plain gray box. A tiny harp dangling from a solid-gold chain shot emerald green and diamond prisms across his plain white ceiling.

"The harp charm is from Ireland, from Dublin. I wanted an Irish harp fit for the most gifted woman I've ever known." He brushed his knuckles over her flawless cheek, brushed away a stray tear.

"Happy tears," she said.

He nodded. "Our conversation from the other day about the night you played 'Danny Boy' brought back good memories. I want this necklace to do the same."

"It brought back good memories for me too." She fingered the necklace. Her eyes shimmered a soft blue velvet. "I haven't bought a piece of clothing or jewelry for myself in months. Thank you."

"I looked for a twenty-three-karat necklace to match your harp, but this was the best I could afford. My salary as a deputy sheriff isn't much, though I plan to work my way up to a position of management." He drew her to him and she rested her cheek against his chest. "Someday I'll buy you a real harp."

He spoke above her, breathing in her floral perfume, citrus and violets and expectation.

"Money isn't important," she said. "I know this gift is from your heart."

She was splendid. She made him feel alive again, brought him out of his sadness. After his fiancée had left him, he'd grieved, focusing on his scars. But a new emotion was rising over the scars, allowing him to become again the man he once was—one of faith, free from cynicism, free to open his heart once more.

They avoided eye contact. The moment held too much emotion for her, for him.

"I know how much your harp meant to you," he murmured. "You once let me in on a secret, that your parents surprised you with a harp for your twelfth birthday. They'd saved money for years to buy the best. A Lyon and Healy harp, correct?"

"You remembered." Her tears came hard, sudden, and she let them.

He soothed her, crooning, rocking her. "You're not alone anymore, Emmanuelle."

Any further conversation was forgotten as she wept. When she withdrew, she wiped at her eyes with the handkerchief he provided. "I'm sorry. I mean, crying was uncalled for and I put you in an awkward—"

"Don't apologize. You're the best thing that's ever happened to me." He swept wisps of hair from her nape and secured the delicate gold chain around her throat, then ushered her to the bathroom mirror. "Dorothy assured me you'd fall in love with this necklace."

At first, Emmanuelle kept her gaze downcast before staring at herself. Carefully, she slid a finger along the fine chain and then found the exquisite detailing of the harp. "I haven't worn anything this pretty in many months. Thanks to you, I'm beginning to feel like a woman again. Someone who matters." Her smile sparkled in the mirror reflection.

He stood behind her and rested his hands on her shoulders. "You matter very, very much. More than you can ever imagine."

He stared at her, a vision of beauty with the heirloom-quality necklace shimmering against her creamy skin above her navy-blue cashmere sweater. At that moment he knew. It had returned, his love for a woman.

Only this time it was real.

*a*fter Dr. Troutman's nod of approval, Nicholas and Emmanuelle set off for the Christmas tree farm. Molly Belle waited in Nicholas's car while they chose the last fir tree on the lot. The tree wasn't perfectly shaped; in fact, it wasn't shaped at all. Nicholas named the tree Charlie Brown since the branches jutted out in random angles.

"Every underdog needs a loving home," he declared, and Emmanuelle wholeheartedly agreed.

One of the employees at the farm shook the tree to remove any loose needles, then wrapped it for transport. A short drive later, Emmanuelle and Nicholas hoisted the scraggly tree up his flight of stairs and into his apartment.

"The tree looks better already," she said as Nicholas secured the tree in a sturdy metal stand. "It's just begging for lots of care and plenty of water. And we'll trim your whole apartment to resemble an old-fashioned Christmas. Ryan's book features all sorts of inspiring ideas."

Nicholas pushed himself to his feet after pouring water into the base of the tree stand. "I thought it was a cookbook focused on recipes."

"Recipes and decorating tips. And there's a thought-provoking article on empowering women that provides tips on how to keep safe in dangerous circumstances. The entire book is highly motivating."

"Quite the cookbook," he observed.

They referenced a "traditional Christmas" article as a guide and spent the afternoon decorating. Using heavy embroidery floss, they strung popcorn and cranberries. Nicholas found a set of multicolored lights stuffed in his hall closet. He began at the tree trunk and moved upward, wrapping the lights taut by weaving them from side to side.

"There isn't much of a tree to light," he said with a laugh. "The branches are beyond sparse!"

"I'm always drawn to these types of trees." She stepped back to assess the tree. "In the end, it's all about hope, isn't it?"

"True. And few people are as hopeful as Charlie Brown."

"Multicolored lights remind me of happy times with my family in Remsen. Call me nostalgic and old-fashioned."

"Then I'm old-fashioned too. Nothing is better than colored lights on a green pine tree to get you in the mood for Christmas."

"Last year, my ex wanted white lights and neon-blue bulbs on the tree he'd purchased for his swanky condo in a high-rise. I argued for colored lights. He didn't agree, of course, saying white lights were chic and modern. I like modern." She hesitated, combed nervous fingers through her hair. "No that's wrong. I just told him that."

"You lied?"

"I had no choice. He had two switches, calm or angry. I knew better than to disagree and kept my opinion to myself. He'd trained me like we're training Molly Belle—to obey commands." She watched the dog, resting on a blanket in the corner. The dog returned her stare with steady, shining eyes.

"I understand my former situation now," she went on. "It's easier at a distance."

"What's your ex's name?"

She took a moment to adjust her fire-red tunic, fussing and fidgeting, as if the tunic didn't fit correctly over her jeans. "George."

"That's it? George? George who?"

"Just George." She shrugged, shivered. Slight, but he saw it.

"Where's George now?"

Another shrug. She looked around, rubbed her hands together. "I assume he's in New York."

Her ex had evidently hurt her, and the realization brought anger bubbling to Nicholas's throat. When he found him, *and he would*, he'd silence George with a good stiff jab and a command of his own. *Stay away from Emmanuelle.*

He wrapped an arm around her shoulders and she leaned into him. Each time they were with each other, his need to protect her grew stronger.

He turned to the next page in the book to change the subject. She might get too upset if they continued discussing her ex. "The next round of decorating is to find red and green bulbs for our quirky tree. Do you prefer glass bulbs or—"

"I prefer family vintage bulbs and pinecones and silver tinsel. But ..." She dug in her tote bag and drew out a tiny angel ornament, brandishing it in the air. "I've carried this with me ever since I left New York. The clerk at the airport told me it was a good luck charm. It belongs on your tree."

"*Our* tree," he corrected her, and hung the ornament on a thin lower branch. "All this decorating warrants a celebration, so let's call out for pizza."

"Again? Is pizza your remedy for everything?"

With a laugh, he pulled his phone from his jeans pocket

and placed an order for a large cheese and pepperoni pizza, with a side of barbecue for Emmanuelle.

After pocketing his phone, he took her hands. "Let's wait for the delivery on the porch steps. The weather is mild, so we can go outside without jackets." He glanced at Molly Belle, sleeping soundly, then eased open the door.

They sat on the stoop. It was one of those inviting South Carolina evenings, when the sun had warmed everything in its path, including his front porch.

The view of his charming cul-de-sac lit with strings of festive lights, the nearby clip-clop of a horse-drawn carriage, filled him with gratitude. He imagined the residents inside their homes, savoring steaming cups of hot cocoa, sitting beside their cozy fireplaces.

From a few streets away came the last strains of "We Three Kings." Sung, he surmised, by the Cherish Church ladies' caroling group. He grinned, envisioning the women, young and elderly, dressed in their traditional Victorian costumes, complete with big bonnets and hand muffs.

The day had been perfect. Ending the evening with Emmanuelle by his side brought a quiet, joyous peace, and he whispered a prayer of thanksgiving. Tenderly, he pressed a kiss on her palms. "Two weeks from today is the Musically Yours holiday concert," he said. "Ryan is leading the elementary school chorus in a Christmas carol singalong and then singing a couple solos."

She rested her cheek on his shoulder. "Cherish is like a picture out of a Christmas card."

He chuckled and went back to appreciating the street decorations. Several neighbors had run animated light displays in a scalloped pattern along their fences.

Yes, this was the ideal town to live, to work, to raise a family.

He put an arm around her and she snuggled nearer, the

warmth of her body reaching out to his. He could get used to this. A delightful woman, her breathing soft and even, whose slight body had grown heavier because she was ... sleeping?

He grinned. She'd fallen asleep quickly, even quicker than he usually did. Between taking care of his dog and creating nightly meals fit for a food connoisseur, she was clearly exhausted. He considered her profile, her small turned-up nose, the light sprinkling of freckles on her cheeks. Several times during the past week, he'd caught her staring at her cell phone as it rang. She never answered a call, and a few times her face had turned bone-white when she'd glimpsed the screen.

"Unknown caller," she always said, dropping the phone back into her tote bag. Whenever he pressed for details, she just chewed her bottom lip and stubbornly stayed silent.

He reached into his pocket for his phone and canceled the pizza. No sense in waking her when the delivery person arrived. Surely that frozen pizza was sitting somewhere in his freezer.

From inside the apartment, Molly Belle barked.

Emmanuelle woke with a start and rubbed her eyes. She peered at him, darted a peek at her watch. "Sorry, I didn't realize I dozed. I haven't rested well in several months."

"Because of George?"

A noticeable gap hung in the air as she scanned the street and its bright decorations. Distractedly, she nodded.

He went to brush pine needles from her shoulder and she flinched. He let out a whistled sigh and pulled back his hand. "Don't. You insult me when you do that."

"Do what?"

"Treat me as if I'm your ex. Just because I raise my hand doesn't mean I'm going to hit you." He deliberated, but only for a second. "What's really going on with you?"

"Too much." She eased up, then sat back down. "Nicholas,

I can't give you the relationship you want. I'm not the right woman for you."

"How do you know?"

She closed her eyes. Tears escaped. "Because you're a good man and my life is complicated."

"I like complicated."

"No, no, you don't." She opened her eyes, a deep shimmery blue. They stared at each other.

"It's odd," he mused.

"What?"

"The fact you're a harpist and you don't have a harp. Did you sell it?"

"My harp was smashed to pieces." She didn't pause for his sympathy, didn't bury her face in her hands. "George destroyed it."

"Why?"

He hadn't meant to ask the question because he knew the answer. As a law enforcement officer, he'd come across men like George. Domestic violence was the leading cause of injury to women. He'd read the statistics, recognized an abuser's behaviors and characteristics. After the honeymoon phase, they became controlling and jealous, and oftentimes sought to isolate their partner.

"Why?" Emmanuelle repeated. "Why would a man who supposedly cared for me take away something I loved, something so meaningful? To break me, I suppose." She shook her head; she'd answered her own question. "He knew precisely which buttons to press. He was exceptionally charming and people were attracted to him. Me included."

Nicholas's anger was sharp. He pulled it in. "How did you meet him?"

"His secretary booked me to play the harp for one of his office functions, the grand opening of his tenth boutique hotel in the New York area." Her voice caught. "After we became a couple, he always reminded me I was beneath him and how thankful I should be an important man like him was interested in someone like me … someone who was little more than a street performer."

"You know that's not true. You're a skilled professional."

She trailed her fingers along the edge of the porch railing and let out a sigh.

"When are you deserting me for New York?" he asked.

"I'm not deserting you. I happen to live there." She smiled and broke off, apparently waiting for his rejoinder. When he didn't offer one, she added, "I don't have a definite date in mind. Dorothy offered me a job at her music conservatory. I've considered finding a place in town and teaching harp lessons." She shrugged and blew out a breath. "Although I know it's better if I keep moving."

The last part of her answer didn't register because he'd fixated on the first part. His heart had leapt when she'd mentioned living in Cherish.

"Is he the reason you came here? Is he the reason you choose to keep running?"

"I have no choice and I'm not running." Her fingers nervously worked the hem of her tunic before she propped her chin in her hands. "Okay, yes, maybe I am. If George O'Donnell finds me, I don't know what he'll do."

George O'Donnell. Piercing rage sliced Nicholas like a knife. "He won't do anything to harm you. I'll make sure of it."

"You don't know him. He's well-off and powerful."

He joined her cold hands with his warm ones. "And I'm in law enforcement."

"That's why I'm afraid. If you go after him, you'll get hurt. He operates in influential circles with big-city types."

"In our quiet town, you'll be safe. You must know I'll always protect you."

"Our town," she repeated.

"Yes. And our life."

"Nicholas?" A smile ghosted her lips as an errant tear streamed down her cheek. "Will you do something for me?"

He gazed at her enchanting face, her over-bright eyes. He would protect her with his life.

"Anything," he said.

"Will you hold me for a minute?"

CHAPTER 9

$\mathcal{I}$n the ensuing two weeks Emmanuelle slept poorly, despite the inn's exquisitely appointed room and her luxurious queen-sized bed. Nightmares chased her and were always the same: the dim outline of a man with flat black eyebrows above dull gray eyes, trailing her every move.

George O'Donnell.

She'd scramble through unnamed woods while the flash of something vicious, and corrupt, and overpowering, followed her. The nightmare always ended the same, with her weeping and running farther and farther away from Cherish.

She'd wake beneath her cozy coverlet, her heart hammering, searching the room for something recognizable. Country-green walls, the hand-stitched quilt draped over a rocking chair, the braided rug covering the wide-plank pine floor, helped steady her breathing.

"Only a nightmare," she'd murmur, wiping her sweaty brow. "Vivid, horrible, and not real."

She'd focus out the window at the sprinkling of stars

against the black velvet sky. Then she'd close her eyes and think about Nicholas—his kindness, his easy-going manner, his self-assured confidence. Efficient and calm, whether tidying his home or ministering to Molly Belle, dealing with dangerous circumstances on duty or holding her as if she were a china doll. He was all man, all kindness, all compassion.

"In our quiet town, you'll be safe. You must know I'll always protect you," he'd said.

Only then, imagining his capable arms around her, could she seek the peace of slumber.

* * *

BY THE THIRD week of December, Cherish had become a jubilant fairyland, a kaleidoscope of Yuletide hues. Parades were held every weekend, and quaint mom-and-pop stores were decked out in magical window dressings. Children and adults alike stopped and gaped, mesmerized in child-like fascination.

Illuminated by tiny white lights, Emmanuelle's comfy inn, with its snow-covered roof and wisps of smoke billowing from the chimney, looked like a postcard image of Christmas town, USA.

Tom had taken a liking to Molly Belle and allowed her inside, provided she stayed in the foyer and didn't jump on any of the patrons. Unfortunately, the third day she was allowed in, Molly Belle knocked a teenage boy over when she'd leapt on the boy's legs. Despite Nicholas's explanations that the dog was still a puppy with a playful, silly personality, Tom banished Molly Belle to the porch. Both hands braced on his polished wood desk, he'd leaned forward until his cheaters slid down his nose and declared she wasn't allowed inside until she graduated from dog obedience school.

Considering Nicholas had abandoned the idea of obedience school until Molly Belle was fully recovered, Emmanuelle was certain the dog wouldn't be entering the inn anytime soon.

A cold front had brought snow to Cherish, a white dusting that topped off the winter-wonderland. As the snow fell softly, day after day, Emmanuelle's mood became more hopeful. She spent her time at Nicholas's apartment caring for Molly Belle and cooking delectable meals—a flaky crusted chicken pot pie brimming with roasted chicken and baby carrots one night, a sweet winter corn-bread with a splash of jalapeno the next. Oftentimes, she'd bake a tray of Christmas cookies, oozing chocolate chips, warm from the oven. As she cooked, she'd tune the radio to a Christian holiday station and hum along to every Christmas carol.

In the middle of the afternoon, she'd leash Molly Belle for a walk. Few things outshone walking a devoted dog who loved going outside for a squirrel-chasing adventure, espe-cially when sunlight warmed Emmanuelle's cheeks and bracing air brought remembrances of Christmas in Remsen.

At Dorothy's prodding, the two women spent an evening shopping. Emmanuelle purchased a pair of shiny gold earrings to complement her harp necklace, plus a rose-tinted lip gloss. There was something so feminine about earrings and lip gloss, Dorothy said, that made a woman feel attrac-tive. Regarding her reflection in the shop's mirror, Emmanuelle agreed. She'd caught her hair at the nape and secured it with a lace bow, the result a messy bun highlighted by escaping corkscrews of blonde hair.

She'd also painted two opposite walls of Nicholas's living room in a golden-yellow and convinced him to reupholster his couch in a deep-chocolate brown. He'd grinned his approval, and she too was pleased with the result. After

Christmas, she aimed to tackle his kitchen and paint those walls a cool mint-green.

After Christmas.

Yes, because she'd decided to live in Cherish. She hadn't told Nicholas, not yet. She'd decided to surprise him on Christmas, after they attended a church service with Dorothy and Ryan. She'd accepted Dorothy's offer to give harp lessons at the Musically Yours music conservatory and had begun formulating a plan to buy a new harp. Ryan told her that the nearby city of Stanley boasted an excellent symphony that was actively looking for a principal harpist, and encouraged her to audition. She'd agreed, the idea prompting recollections of how much she enjoyed performing.

On the Saturday of the holiday concert in Cherish, Emmanuelle spent the morning peeling potatoes and carrots for a hearty beef stew she simmered on Nicholas's stove. The weatherman had predicted snow, which had rapidly accumulated to several inches.

Nicholas had had to respond to a domestic-dispute call, and she'd gladly volunteered to stay with Molly Belle. He'd added that one of the other officers, Joseph Hannaford, would be on duty at the concert that evening. Large crowds were expected because of Ryan Edwards's performance.

Done with the stew, she surveyed the living room from the kitchen doorway. The Charlie Brown Christmas tree was delightful, brightly lit and brimming with cheer. Her angel ornament hung from one of the branches, and she laughed out loud, inhaling the scents of pine and promise.

Life was good. Very good. On an even more optimistic note, there'd been no sign of George. After she'd begun watching Molly Belle, every morning she'd received a phone call precisely at eight o'clock, a few minutes after Nicholas left for work.

Whenever she answered, no one spoke.

Once, she'd sworn she'd heard breathing on the other end. Bad connection? Most likely. She rejected her suspicions that it might be George. Merely an over-zealous telemarketer, she'd tell herself.

Still, she told Nicholas, admitting to her uneasiness. He listened thoughtfully before assuring her she was right—a telemarketer had programmed her phone number on speed-dial. After a long, thorough kiss, he assured her there was nothing to worry about.

And then, without warning, the mysterious phone calls had stopped.

As the next few days passed, the realization she was finally free from George renewed her confidence. With a strong handsome deputy by her side, friends who loved her, and a spirited dog ever near, what was there to fear? Truly, Christmas in Cherish promised a happiness she'd never dreamed.

CHAPTER 10

*a*fter they'd eaten stew for an early dinner, Nicholas drove Emmanuelle back to the inn to get ready for the evening concert. They passed tree limbs heavy with snow, bushes dusted with a fine white powder.

At the inn, she gifted Tom with a loaf of her crusty bread, prompting him to taste it. He'd chewed with his eyes closed and exclaimed, "Will you marry me, Emmanuelle?"

Before she could reply, Nicholas draped an arm on her shoulders and assured the innkeeper she was spoken for.

She floated to her room where she ran a warm shower, refreshing herself under a stream of multiple jets. The scents of her soap and shampoo—brown sugar and vanilla—reminded her of hot cinnamon rolls slathered in butter cream frosting.

Her anticipation of the evening rising, she grabbed a fluffy towel for her hair, and wrapped herself in a luxurious white robe. She padded across the wood floor of her room and deliberated on her outfit, ultimately choosing a comfortable pair of colored denims and a red cashmere sweater.

Despite his numerous concert engagements, she'd never

heard Ryan perform live, and she was looking forward to the evening.

At 7:00, a light tap on her door signaled Nicholas's arrival.

When she opened the door, he lifted her to her toes and held her. "Emmanuelle Sumter, you look gorgeous and smell like a cinnamon roll." He frequently remarked on her appearance, always complimentary, always causing her to melt, just melt.

She saw the seductive-green passion in his hazel eyes as their lips met.

"And every time I see you," he went on, "I fall more in love with you." He stated his feelings simply, without preamble or fanfare, his mouth brushing against her ear, his warm breath heating her insides.

She ran her fingers over his nape. His blond hair was thick and curled over his collared parka. His lips were smooth, his mouth perfectly shaped. His well-defined jaw and sharp cheekbones brought a chiseled handsomeness to his cover model features.

It's too soon to talk of love, she wanted to say. But it wasn't too soon, because she was falling in love with him too.

She hugged the realization close. This good-looking, conscientious man loved her, and with each heartfelt embrace, each heady kiss, her defenses were thawing. Slowly, she was shaking off her fears and yielding to him.

"Ready for an amazing concert?" he asked.

"I can't wait." She went to her closet and tugged a pink tasseled hat over her hair. "Dorothy said she'd accompany Ryan on keyboard if they can figure out how to run electrical power on stage."

"So far, they haven't," Nicholas said. As she rummaged through the closet, he added that the afternoon sun had melted much of the morning's snow, so the streets were messy tonight.

"Just let me grab my boots. Where's Molly Belle?"

"She's near the porch."

She swiveled. "Alone?"

"She's on her leash. Tom is playing with her in the snow." Nicholas struggled to keep a straight face. "He won't admit he's got a soft spot for dogs, although you and I know he does." He helped her on with her jacket and exaggeratedly hefted her tote bag from the bureau. "What do you carry in this? Lead?"

"Necessities. You know, my cell phone, wallet, loose change …"

"I wouldn't want to tote this heavy bag around."

"You would if you were a sensible woman." She laughed. "I can't be deprived of my pink lip gloss."

Still bantering, they made their way down the carpeted staircase.

As soon as they strolled onto the porch, Molly Belle scampered around them, feathery tail wagging, as if she hadn't seen them in a month. Nicholas thanked Tom and reached for the leash. Hand in hand, Emmanuelle and Nicholas stepped from the porch.

Although the morning snow had blown in quick and heavy, as Nicholas had said, most had melted under sun-kissed daytime skies. As the evening thermometer plunged, what was left had frozen, causing thin sheets of ice to gloss over the surface of the remaining snow. Tom had shoveled a generous path and covered the steps and sidewalk with rock salt.

"I've never listened to opera," Nicholas said, tucking her hand in the crook of his arm as they started for the town square. "I expect—"

"You've never heard Ryan sing?" Her lips twitched with

amusement. "Your sister is married to one of the most famous opera singers in the world!"

"Once, maybe, when we were teenagers, I overheard him singing an operatic version of Dorothy's favorite top-forty hit. I assumed he was trying to impress her. They used to sit for hours on the side porch of our house." Nicholas's deep voice vibrated with laughter. "But I'm all for the idea of a bonfire and roasting s'mores after the concert."

When they reached the square, Ryan and Dorothy gave an absent-minded wave as they arranged chairs beneath a white canvas tent. A stage had been set up alongside the ten-foot decorated Christmas tree. Various kiosks serving refreshments lined the outer edges of the square, and Nicholas briefly introduced her to his coworker, Joseph Hannaford, the officer on duty. As the crowds thickened, a fine, snowy mist began to fall.

A halcyon town awaiting Christmas, Emmanuelle mused. The entire scene was a miniature version of New York's festive theater district. Cheery memories, she thought, … until … until …

She brought a jittery hand to her forehead.

A few months after she began dating George, she wore her favorite sweater to a theater event, and had left her jacket in the restroom at intermission. When he noticed, he demanded they leave before the show was over. She assumed he was angry because she had been foolish enough to have forgotten her jacket. He was concerned, as the theater was cold, she reasoned.

She was way off the mark. He shouted at her and called her a tramp for strutting around in a clingy sweater that he deemed too provocative.

He was jealous. She got that, and even felt flattered.

At first.

The relationship deepened. She believed she was in love

with him, and he was in love with her. However, he began to erupt when she least expected, no matter how fine a line she walked. Scary remembrances of George's viciousness, his narcissistic behavior, his insincere repentance, brought a quake down her spine.

She forced the chilling memories away and glanced at the rugged man standing beside her.

She was being foolish. She was safe, the town was real, this man was real. And this was the picture she needed to carry in order to move forward in her life. The uncommonly large crowd had simply dredged up memories from her uneasy mind.

As if he'd read her thoughts, Nicholas protectively tightened his arm around her waist. "Are you all right?" His hazel gaze locked on hers.

"Yes, I was thinking about how grateful I am to be here. And I'm happy, truly happy."

"So am I." He spoke quietly, tenderly. "I love you, Emmanuelle."

She beamed up at him, this man of faith whom she'd enjoyed endless conversations with, a man who spoke plainly what was on his heart.

"I love you too, Nicholas."

He smiled at her as if she were incredibly beloved.

She sighed with contentment. Finally, her world was coming together, and she whispered a thank you to God for giving her a promising future alongside the man she loved.

As they wove through the tent to find a good seat, she scanned the tent to see where Dorothy and Ryan had gone.

An exuberant Dorothy was arranging the last row of folding chairs. Her simple, classic black sweater dress showed off every curve of her lithe figure. She'd pinned her dark hair into an understated twist at the back of her head, drawing attention to her emerald-green eyes and pearl stud earrings.

Ryan strode over to her, impressively tall with dark, compelling features, his broad shoulders filling out his navy jacket to perfection. He draped a tweed coat around Dorothy. Something she said made him laugh out loud, and he gathered her in his arms and kissed her.

Their delight in each other was so infectious that Nicholas and Emmanuelle shared a grin.

"Well?" he prompted.

"Well what?"

"Well, if everyone is kissing, then where's my kiss?"

"You're impossible. We're not performing in a concert tonight."

"I plan to sing along to every Christmas carol. Does that count?"

She chuckled. "No. Besides, we're not newlyweds."

"Not yet." A slow, roguish smile moved across his face.

She felt her blood heat from her toes to her temple. "You're thinking to kiss me here, with all these people around?" Coyly, she shook her head, teasingly discouraging him. Then with a mischievous smile, she tilted her head back, inviting a kiss.

Dr. Troutman and Scarlett entered the tent carrying two cups of coffee and a bag of chips. They spotted them, waved, and jostled through the crowd. Molly Belle yipped and tugged on her leash in her attempt at a greeting.

Her red hair springy beneath her leopard ear muffs, Scarlett offered a sparkling smile and opened her chips. She offered them to the group, then began munching.

"How's one of my favorite dogs?" Dr. Troutman rubbed Molly Belle's head as she scrabbled her front paws up his legs. He bent and examined her feet. "Just making sure there's no snow trapped in the pads."

"I've been checking," Emmanuelle said.

He sipped his coffee. "Are you two here for the concert?"

"*I* am," Emmanuelle said and then pointed to Nicholas. "He's here for the s'mores."

Dr. Troutman made a dramatic show of choking on his coffee. "Glad to see you're still in Cherish, Emmanuelle. Don't you live in New York?"

Nicholas pressed a light kiss on her forehead. "I'm trying to talk her into moving permanently to Cherish."

"Well, I could use a knowledgeable person in my office. Scarlett is a wonderful receptionist although she's going to be a little busy, now that we're engaged." His hand reached out to cover Scarlett's, but not before Emmanuelle noticed a three-stone diamond ring in a rose-gold setting on Scarlett's ring finger.

"Congratulations," Emmanuelle and Nicholas said simultaneously.

"Thank you." Scarlett's shimmery, ruby earrings swung sideways as she nodded. Enthusiasm glowing in her face, she turned to Dr. Troutman. "I love animals, but I love you more."

Emmanuelle saw the elation in the veterinarian's smile as he swung his attention back toward her. "If you're looking for a job, Emmanuelle, you can work for me anytime."

"My sister beat you to it." Nicholas said, nodding toward Dorothy. "She asked Emmanuelle to teach music lessons at her conservatory. Did you know Emmanuelle is a professional harpist?"

"I'd like to hear you play," Scarlett said.

"Someday." Emmanuelle grimaced. How's that for evasive? she upbraided herself. She was a professional harpist with no harp.

"I'm sorry. I can see from the expression on your face that

I troubled you." Scarlett swallowed a chip and snapped up another. "Dorothy mentioned you don't have a harp."

Emmanuelle stopped her grimace and turned it into a smile. "Don't apologize. Look what Nicholas bought me. Isn't it beautiful?" She drew out the harp necklace from beneath her jacket for Scarlett to admire.

"Yes, very beautiful, and very thoughtful." Scarlett eyed the necklace. "An early Christmas gift, Nicholas?"

"Nope." He laughed. "It's my gift to Emmanuelle for coming to Cherish. She's a blessing to me."

Emmanuelle's heart gave a funny lurch. Nicholas offered safety and security and he was more considerate than anyone she'd ever known. Not every man was cruel and intimidating, she reminded herself yet again. Healing from abuse was a slow road, and it took time and infinite perseverance. And she'd walk that road with the man she loved.

New beginnings.

"You make a very striking couple," Scarlett was saying. "Two good-looking blondes."

"I agree with one of your observations." With a mile-wide beam toward Emmanuelle, Nicholas said, "We'd better claim a seat, my good-looking blonde."

As people converged, aromas of chocolate fudge and honey roasted almonds lifted into the air.

"The staid doctor and his perky receptionist are engaged?" Emmanuelle asked.

"Apparently." He grinned. "He must be twice her age."

"They're charming together and I'm delighted for them."

"The vet has lived alone on his alpaca farm since his wife's passing. He's a moral Christian man and I'm glad he met someone he can share his life with."

"I hope Scarlett likes alpacas." Emmanuelle laughed. "Do they bite?"

"Not normally. And she can eat her junk food while Dr. Troutman's alpaca herd munches on green plants and grass."

They settled on seats in the last row, just in case Molly Belle spotted another dog and attempted to dash off for an impromptu romp in the snow.

When the audience quieted, the first half of the concert began with the elementary school's children's chorus. The music teacher conducted, and everyone joined in a heart-lifting rendition of "Silent Night." Before intermission, Ryan led the crowd in the "Hallelujah" chorus from Handel's *Messiah*. As tradition dictated, everyone stood.

"I've always wondered," Nicholas said under his breath, "why are we supposed to stand?"

"There are many theories, the principal one being that King George II was so overwhelmed by the 'Hallelujah' chorus that he stood up. And whenever the king stood, so did everyone else."

After a brief intermission, Ryan came on stage for the second half. His bass voice, rich and finely textured, was exactly as Dorothy had described, and Emmanuelle felt as if she couldn't breathe during his entire a cappella rendition of "Away in a Manger."

When the concert finished to thunderous clapping, whistles, and cheers, Ryan held up a hand to quell the applause and extended congratulations to the children's chorus. The children scampered back on stage, bowed low, and then grinned and waved at the audience.

Emmanuelle rose along with Nicholas and announced she'd ferret out the booths serving roasted almonds and fudge. Her nose could only take so much temptation.

He circled an arm around her shoulders. "What about our s'mores? The mayor is building the bonfire and we'll eat in a few minutes."

"I'm adopting Scarlett's motto—to embrace life and

indulge yourself. No worries. I promise I'll eat the fudge and almonds and s'mores." She sighed. "Although I won't be able to fit into the holiday skirt I brought if I keep eating at this rate. Fortunately, I also own a pair of slacks with an elastic waist."

Nicholas didn't appease her with a chuckle. Instead, his fingers tightened on her shoulders. "I'll go with you."

"Why?"

"Those suspicious phone calls you were getting …" He looked around and nodded at a busload of fans swarming around Ryan. "There're too many people here tonight."

"I'm twenty-five, not five, and I lived in New York, one of the busiest cities in the world. I can certainly navigate a crowd and get my own snacks without an escort. I'm over my fear of walking alone." She shook off his arm and grabbed her tote bag. "Besides, Dorothy's headed our way. Please congratulate her for me. I'll shoot ahead of this next horde and catch up with all of you in a few minutes."

He hesitated. "Are you certain you'll be okay?"

"Enough time has passed. I'm better. Really." She walked purposefully toward the food kiosks. Out from under the tent, she saw the night was black—no moon or stars, and the shimmer of snow was now a gray mist.

She wound past the busy fudge and caramel-corn stands. The stand that advertised roasted almonds was farther down, and there was no line. Actually, the stand looked deserted. Had they sold out of almonds already and closed shop?

She paused, debating what to do, and sensed someone walking up behind her. "Emmanuelle," a man said, "can you give me directions to the stage?

She was so sure she'd imagined the familiar voice, she started walking toward the stand.

"Emmanuelle."

She froze. Her shoulders tightened, her breathing stopped. *Move*, she commanded her feet.

"Turn around, Emmanuelle."

Obediently, she did. George had always had a hold over her.

The sight of him standing so near was enough to unfreeze her. She shifted, one foot stepping back, but his gaze immediately sharpened on her. If only she could make him believe she was standing stock-still while she slowly moved backward.

"How ... how did you find me?" She licked her lips and expelled a quick breath. He couldn't be here. He was locked away in a hidden compartment in her mind, in New York, at a theater festival.

"Didn't take long." He grabbed her arm. "A couple of your so-called friends mentioned you'd gone off to some back-water town in South Carolina for the holidays." He laughed derisively. "'Cherish.' I couldn't even find it on a map."

"You don't know any of my friends." She braced her body against a cold wind and tried not to inhale. He smelled of vodka and anger and day-old sweat.

Despite herself, she couldn't control the shiver that rippled through her. He noticed. She saw the satisfaction in his bloodshot gray eyes. He had foreseen this, her cowering, her clumsiness, as she fingered the straps of her tote bag.

"I hired a few musicians for my office party," he said. His fingers tightened on her arm and she flinched. "They were more than willing to help once I offered a large bonus. You starving performers are always looking for handouts."

She swallowed a terrified scream and eyed her isolated surroundings. Several long sprints lay between her and the roasted-almond stand. She could outrun him.

No, argued her practical self. He was a large man. His pace outmatched hers, and he'd overtake her. All he'd have to do was drag her into the nearby woods, and she'd be alone with him.

Adrenaline consumed her, shaping her terror into a soundless rage. She wasn't a weak, passive victim, shrinking into herself just because he spoke.

This was her town, not his.

Mentally, she reviewed the article from the *Southern Charms* cookbook. If a woman was confronted by an attacker, one of her first lines of defense was her handbag.

She lifted her chin, straightened her spine. "Well, now that you've seen for yourself I'm here, go slither back to your swanky place in New York."

Momentarily, his composure slipped, his fingers loosened. "Every day, I think about when your broken harp was hauled away. I felt so bad, I decided to buy you a new one. We'll call it my Christmas gift to you. It's expensive. You'll like it."

"Keep it. I don't want it."

His eyebrows lifted in distracted mockery. "What—"

She couldn't be afraid. She couldn't allow herself to cringe and plead, but needed to prevent her fright from taking over.

Don't back away. Use the element of surprise. He won't expect you to fight.

"I said keep it." She lifted her heavy tote bag as a club and swung directly for his face.

She was too slow. He saw the blow coming and shoved her to the ground. A dull roar filled her ears, pain firing through her body as she hit solid ice. He fell on top of her, and she fought him, biting and kicking, jabbing at his eyes, focusing all her energy on getting away.

A shiny, silver knife sliced the air and came at her throat. "I heard you've been seeing an officer in town, Emmanuelle. Did you forget? You were meant only for me."

She shut her eyes to keep out the light-headedness, seeking the safety of somewhere dark and safe and silent.

Heavy, racing footsteps cut through her dizzying thoughts.

"Drop the knife and keep your hands over your head."

"George O'Donnell, you're under arrest for aggravated assault."

Two men's voices. Nicholas. And another man. Officer Joseph Hannaford.

"Emmanuelle? Are you okay?" Nicholas's steady tone reached through her fogged thoughts. She squinted. The color had drained from his face, and even in the darkness she could see his distress.

Tears welled. "Yes, yes. I'm—I'm fine. He didn't hurt ..."

Her brave declaration was diminished by her sobbing. She couldn't contain her tears and reached out to Nicholas for comfort. She wanted to be held, wanted her apprehension quieted, wanted only him. Her legs wobbled as he helped her to her feet, and she sagged against his strong body. His gaze stayed focused on her.

George sneered at her as Officer Hannaford snapped handcuffs on him. "You won't get away with this, Emmanuelle."

She noted that he showed no remorse.

"I already did," she said flatly. "Quit following me and go back to New York. I never want to see you again."

"This one stop-light town is no fun. I was leaving anyway." He didn't look tough or threatening now, not with his hands cuffed behind his back. "Just remember, Emmanuelle. You're an insignificant nobody."

Nicholas tightened his fists. "What did you say, O'Donnell?"

"Nothing, Nicholas," she said quickly. "He can't hurt me anymore."

The slow dance of George's belittlement, his cruelty, had ended. His hurtful comments would no longer snake through her dreams because she refused to carry her resentment anymore. She'd acted with courage, and someday, with God's grace, she'd forgive George. Just not today.

"Mr. O'Donnell," Officer Hannaford said, "we've been monitoring your activities. Lots of illegal narcotics are being siphoned through your hotel deliveries into other states besides New York. Drug trafficking is a felony, a federal one when it's across state lines. And then there's the evidence of money laundering, illegal weapons, and other crimes." His gaze flicked to Emmanuelle, then zeroed in on Nicholas's clenched fists. "Why don't you bring your girl back to your apartment and cool off? I guarantee this guy will be locked away for a good many years."

CHAPTER 11

$\mathcal{E}$mmanuelle looked like a dream and cooked like a gourmet chef, Nicholas decided, taking a whiff of something heavenly as he strode into his apartment. He was greeted by Molly Belle's hopeful eyes and madly flapping tail.

He hung his pea coat by the door, took off his deputy badge, and slid the gun from his holster. With the dog on his heels, he locked the gun in his safe.

"No walks, Molly Belle," he said. "Emmanuelle texted me and I know you've been outside twice already."

Molly Belle cocked her silky ears, then followed him into the kitchen.

Nicholas feasted his gaze on Emmanuelle as she blended ingredients for a holiday fruitcake. She was dressed for Christmas Eve in a red velvet top and black pencil skirt that showed off her perfectly toned legs. She'd tied a plaid apron featuring a gingerbread man over her outfit. Her blonde hair tumbled in ringlets around her shoulders.

"Merry Christmas, angel," he said. "You're stunning." He tried not to stare, but she sure had shapely legs. He'd brought home a bouquet of red and white carnations, a festive beginning to the Christmas season, the florist had declared, when she'd snatched his credit card and rung up the sale.

No matter how hard he tried to budget, money seemed to slip out of his fingers faster than water.

"Well, thank you, Deputy Thompson," Emmanuelle said. "You're quite handsome yourself in your deputy uniform." She wiped a hand on her apron and twirled. "I was able to squeeze into this skirt after all, despite the endless barbecue sandwiches I've eaten lately. How do I look?"

"Gorgeous." He grinned approvingly, then held up the flowers.

Her face lit. "For me?"

"For Ryan and Dorothy's house," he amended. "The carnations are a Christmas dinner centerpiece, a thank you gift to them along with your ... fruitcake." He gave himself a silent pat on the back for not grimacing.

He blamed his fruitcake dislike on the media, for the cake was fodder for endless jokes. His favorite was one by Johnny Carson, "There is only one fruitcake in the entire world, and people keep sending it to each other."

He didn't share that quote with Emmanuelle.

"I'm trying a new recipe," she said. "This one was passed down to Ryan by his nana."

"Yes, you'd mentioned it this morning. No *Southern Charms* recipe?"

"This one is better." Emmanuelle grinned and pressed the mixture into a baking pan. "It's so generous of your sister and Ryan to welcome us into their new home for the holidays."

The air smelled subtly of candied cherries and walnuts and dates, and Nicholas sniffed enthusiastically. Should he give fruitcake another chance? Most likely, Emmanuelle's cake would prove as tasty as all the other delicacies she'd prepared the past few weeks.

He set the bouquet on the table and brought her into his arms for a hello kiss.

"I missed you today." He nuzzled her neck. The splendid-ness of her, her sweet lips pressed to his, her sylphlike form leaning into him, brought him such happiness.

She wiped her hands on her apron and twined her arms around him. When he didn't release her, she shifted. "The fruitcake," she reminded him.

"Fruitcakes are invincible." He kept her close and rested his chin on her shiny blonde curls.

"Nicholas ..." She extracted herself to pop the cake into the oven. "The recipe says the cake takes forty-five minutes to bake, which gives us plenty of time to arrive at Dorothy and Ryan's house by seven for dinner. The church service starts at midnight." She glanced at her watch. "It's five now."

Absently, he rubbed Molly Belle's head and eyeballed Emmanuelle as she pulled off her apron and put the flowers in a vase with water.

"Nicholas, did you hear me?"

"I think so."

"What did I say?"

"Something about Christmas dinner." He'd heard the dinner part and little else. He'd been preoccupied with her gorgeous legs.

"I brewed a pot of coffee. Do you want a cup?"

Before he answered, she brought out two mugs from his glass-front cabinet and poured.

"No donuts?" he teased, rousing her into a smile.

"On Christmas we eat fruitcake for dessert."

He sighed and scratched his head. *How could he forget?* He'd just have to keep hoping for the best.

"Emmanuelle ..." From his shirt pocket, he withdrew a neatly wrapped present tied with a white satin bow. "This is a little gift I bought for you."

She looked surprised. "You're very generous, but my wonderful harp necklace is more than enough."

Which, he'd noticed, she wore every day.

"This is another gift because it's Christmas. And because I appreciate you."

Ever since she'd arrived, his apartment had been transformed. Maybe he hadn't paid attention to the dog hair accumulating on his unswept floors before, but he'd sure appreciated it when his wooden floors gleamed.

She smiled. "I bought gifts for you too. They're wrapped and under our Charlie Brown tree. Let's open them now."

With the dog at their side and coffee cups in hand, they wandered into the living room. She clicked on her favorite Christian radio station, then brought a gold-foil-wrapped box from beneath the tree and handed it to him. "Merry Christmas, Nicholas."

They sat together on the floor, backs against the wall, and stretched out their legs. She was barefoot, free from the restrictions of her former lifestyle—one of control and fear. Now, her smile came easy, her movements unrestrained. The subdued colors of the Christmas tree lights warmed her complexion to a healthy rose hue.

Molly Belle settled beside them, patient, good, eyeing them thoughtfully with shiny black eyes.

Nicholas chuckled. He felt like a kid again, filled with the magic of the season. He felt like singing out loud when a new artist's rendition of "O Come All Ye Faithful" lilted from the radio.

"Well? Why are you waiting?" she teased. Expectantly, she watched him open her gift, an electric travel mug. "Do you like it?"

"I love it. Thank you." He shouted with laughter. "This is perfect."

She grinned. "Now that you're a deputy, you're always

focused on getting a good cup of coffee. If duty calls and pulls you away from the office, your coffee won't be left cold anymore."

"Thank you. I've become attached to my coffee. And I've become even more attached to you." He pressed a kiss to her temple.

Still grinning, she reached behind the tree and produced another box, this one lighter and wrapped in the same metallic-gold foil paper.

"Two gifts?" he asked. "Why?"

"You bought me two, so now we're even." She placed the box on his lap, her expression growing serious.

He unwrapped the foil paper slowly, revealing a large jeweler's box. Then he paused, regarding her for a long moment, wondering why she'd lowered her head and seemed suddenly self-conscious. He unhooked the lid, and a silver pendant hanging from a heavy chain shone back at him.

"Read the words on the front," she encouraged. "It's a prayer."

"All right." He read aloud. "'Lord, keep my deputy safe from morning till night, give him strength in your precious light.'" He turned the pendant over. She'd personalized the back with an engraved script: "'I'm proud of you.'"

He wiped at his eyes as the emotion swept over him. He swallowed and held the pendant up to the light to admire it. "Thank you, Emmanuelle."

"You're very welcome."

He nodded toward his gift. "Now it's your turn."

Her fingers moved more slowly. She set the wrapping paper on the floor and gazed at the silver case she'd revealed. Carefully, she unsnapped the lid. A black velvet bed held a solitaire diamond ring in a twist of fourteen-karat white gold.

She drew an unsteady breath. "It's ... it's beautiful." Tears welled, falling down her cheeks. She wiped at them, laughed as she brushed the wetness away. "These are happy tears," she clarified, laughing and crying at the same time before she sank her head into his chest and gave in to the weeping.

"I know." He held her until her cry had passed. The same joy had gripped him.

Taking her left hand, he slid the diamond engagement ring onto her finger. "Will you marry me, Emmanuelle?"

She stared at her finger, stared at him. "Read the explanation on the box that came with your pendant first."

He gazed at her and pondered her reply. How had the conversation shifted to *her* gift when she wore *his* gift on her finger? If his feelings weren't in such a tangle because she was sitting so close to him, because it was Christmas, because it was so easy to love life again, he would have noticed how her bright eyes shone with anticipation.

He lifted the box and read the inside flap. "'A deputy's wife's prayer.'" He set the box down. Paused. Reflected. "Wait a minute. A *wife's* prayer?"

"I planned on making my home in Cherish, and wanted to tell you on Christmas Eve." She looked almost sheepish. "Then I decided that if you didn't ask me to marry you, I'd ask you."

"Well, my answer is yes." He smothered a laugh and tipped up her face. "What's your answer?"

"Yes, yes, yes. I love you, Nicholas Thompson."

His mouth descended on hers as she pressed closer. "I love you so much," he murmured, and then his mouth captured hers again for a breathtakingly long kiss.

When the kiss ended, she stayed in his arms.

"I've been thinking," she began, snuggling closer.

He brushed a kiss against her hair. "About what?"

"About the past few days, going over and over what happened the night of the concert. You obviously knew my relationship with George wasn't over. I didn't. And then I fought back when he attacked me. I shouldn't have."

"He's a dangerous man. You didn't realize how dangerous."

She blew out a breath. "Afterward, when I thought about how deserted it was back there, I chastised myself. I reacted foolishly for edging him on, and then trying to fight him."

"It was a knee-jerk reaction. You were threatened. You didn't realize how serious the situation would become, and so quickly. Officer Hannaford and I had been running a long background check on George O'Donnell ever since you told me his last name, so I was at fault. I knew how dangerous he was and I should never have let you go off alone."

"I only walked across the square to buy almonds." She sighed. "Although I've been blaming myself. I'm good at that."

"Don't." He kissed her again. "If anyone is responsible, it's me. I knew that George was involved in illegal activities."

She nodded. "And then I thought, through the bad came the good. Because of you—because of me—because of us, I've taken my power back. I didn't deserve his violence, and I felt so bitter and resentful when I arrived in Cherish. I've prayed a lot, and I finally realized if I kept feeling that way, that meant he still controlled me. So, I've let go of it. New beginnings, thanks to the grace of God."

Nicholas knuckled a tear from the corner of her eye.

She'd confronted her shame, her anger at herself, and realized God had helped her through the storm.

Love was here, love was now. Love was the magic of the season. They were standing on the edge of Christmas, waiting for the new year and their new life to begin.

For an eternity, they sat together on the floor, his arms enveloping her and holding her close.

* * *

NICHOLAS AWOKE to the sound of Molly Belle's whining as she darted across the living room. The shriek of the smoke alarm had him staring blindly ahead. Smoke rolled out of the kitchen.

"Emmanuelle." He shook her awake. "Are you keeping tabs on the time?"

"Yes, it's—" She gaped at her watch. "It's nearly seven o'clock!"

They raced to the kitchen just in time to extract a burnt fruitcake from the oven.

He shut off the smoke alarm. She winced at the cake.

"Oh no." She blew out a breath. "I hope I have enough ingredients left over to bake another one."

"You mean you're going to try to bake another fruitcake?"

She scanned the counter. "Unfortunately, it's too late tonight."

"Well, there's always tomorrow, although none of the stores will be open on Christmas, so we'll just have to wait."

He tried to sound regretful and knew he didn't.

He opened a kitchen window to let out the smoke and inhaled crisp winter air. A neighbor was inching his car into the driveway, wheels spinning, windshield wipers flapping like a wild bird's wings. Fresh snow was falling to the ground, hugging the landscape in a burst of white potential.

"We may not be going anywhere tonight," Emmanuelle murmured. She stood beside him, peering outside the window.

"What will we eat for Christmas dinner?" he asked.

"Burnt fruitcake and coffee?"

"I'll call Dorothy. Once the roads are plowed, we should be able to get to their house and then attend the midnight church service."

He hugged her. The exquisite feeling of her warm body next to his, made his heart beat stronger. He'd been bitter, just like her. In his bitterness, he hadn't wanted to change. He'd preferred to feed on his own loneliness and feel sorry for himself. And then, God had blessed him with Emmanuelle. He'd brought her into his life at the perfect time.

She was his family now, along with Dorothy and Ryan. And Molly Belle, who'd trotted into the kitchen, plopped beneath the kitchen table and curiously eyed the burnt fruitcake.

By the window, Nicholas kissed Emmanuelle, a kiss full of love and promise. "I love you, Emmanuelle."

Her eyes were wet with tears. "I love you too."

"And I'll take a lifetime to prove it to you, right here in Cherish," he said.

"You don't have to prove anything. I know the man you are, and that's why I love you."

Truly, whatever came their way, they could handle it. His faith had been tested, but these were lessons. He'd bounced back from sadness and adversity. They'd both bounced back.

Because God had them covered. Together and always.

With Emmanuelle in his arms, they were ready to face life's challenges.

And this was a Christmas to cherish.

THE END

A NOTE FROM JOSIE

Dear Friends,

Thank you for reading *A Christmas To Cherish* and spending time in the fictional town of Cherish, South Carolina.

I have always loved small-town life, and writing this story felt like a natural gift to give both myself and my readers. Because I am a musician and played the harp for a time, I gave that joy to Emmanuelle. There is a quality to harp music that is both fragile and deeply moving, and I wanted her instrument to reflect the woman herself.

Nicholas first appeared in A Love Song To Cherish as Dorothy's devoted brother, and I simply could not let him go without his own happily ever after. I hope you agree he deserved it.

Cherish has grown into a full series, and if this story resonated with you, I think you will enjoy the others. You can find all six book on Amazon listed below.

If you have a moment, a review on Amazon means the world to an author and helps other readers find their way to Cherish.

A Christmas To Cherish is available in ebook, paperback, large print, hardcover, and audiobook.

I'd love to meet you in person someday, but in the meantime, all I can offer is a sincere and grateful thank you. Without your support, my books would not be possible.

As I write my next sweet or inspirational romance, remember this: Have you ever tried something you were afraid to try because it mattered so much to you? I did, when I started writing. Take the chance, and just do something you love.

My Spotify Play List for A Christmas To Cherish is here.

With appreciation,
Josie Riviera

Love sweet and inspirational holiday romances? Check out these boxed sets:

Holiday Hearts Book Bundle Volume One
Holiday Hearts Book Bundle Volume Two
Holiday Hearts Book Bundle Volume Three
Holiday Hearts Book Bundle Volume Four
Holiday Hearts Book Bundle Volume Five

Want more of the inspirational Cherish series?
Cherish Series.

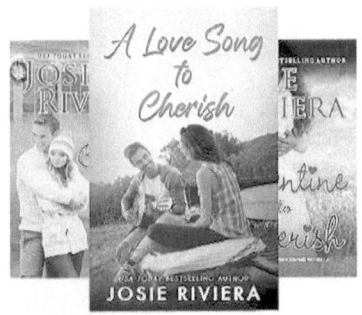

Or grab Cherished Hearts.

The entire series! 6 sweet, inspirational romances in 1 giant boxed set.

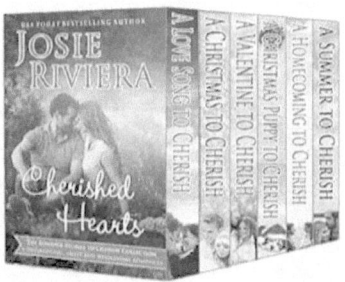

NANA'S FRUITCAKE RECIPE

Ingredients:

4 eggs

1 cup flour

2 teaspoons baking powder

1 pound candied pineapple

1 pound pitted dates

1 pound candied cherries

8 cups walnuts

Instructions:

Pour flour and baking powder into a large paper bag, shake to mix, then add fruits and nuts. Shake well to coat all pieces with flour.

In a large bowl, beat eggs. Pour the fruits and nuts mixture into the egg mixture and use your hand to mix well. Coat all pieces. Grease a small baking pan and press the mixture firmly into the pan. Bake approximately 45 minutes at 350 degrees or until golden brown.

Enjoy!

CHAPTER ONE

Scarlett Evans eyed Joanna, the skinny girl sitting beside her on the wooden park bench. The girl's legs were drawn up to her chest, her limp brown hair parted to the side and pulled into a ponytail. As always, her hair was tangled, as if she'd forgotten about the process of grooming in the middle of the activity.

Scarlett gathered her face into a sunny smile. "Good thing the rain stopped, Joanna."

"Are we going to Dr. Troutman's alpaca farm?" the girl asked.

"He put his farm up for sale last month, remember? There's someone else taking care of the property now, one of his former employees." Scarlett sighed, preferring to forget the slim sandy-haired man who had stolen her heart and then moved away. They'd been in love, or so she'd assumed. Sure, he'd been twice her age and she'd been warned about having a boyfriend twenty years her senior. But he was self-assured and successful, a noteworthy departure from the insecure twenty-something men she had previously dated.

In the end, though, Judson Troutman didn't want to get married again after losing his first wife, nor did he want to be raising a child in his sixties. At least, that's what he'd divulged the day before his departure when he'd broken their engagement.

Children. A family. That resounding black hole between them.

And, he'd admitted, he'd grown tired of Scarlett's loud, boisterous manner.

Since then, she'd attempted to be quieter, more subdued. Messy and spontaneous? These were fixable traits. Disorganized and overweight? Well, she was working on it.

"I thought you liked alpacas," Joanna said.

"The farm wasn't mine, and it was his choice. I love animals, but truthfully, an entire pasture full of alpacas was more than I could handle by myself. My new job learning how to train service dogs at Canine Helpers is wonderfully rewarding, so at least I'm still working with animals." Scarlett heard the hollow emptiness eddying between her excuses. The alpaca farm would have been perfect and she'd counted on it.

Restlessly, she fiddled with her bright-red shoulder bag.

How foolish to believe that a well-educated veterinarian could fall for a woman like her. A woman who wasn't polished. A woman who was too brash and flamboyant for his refined taste.

Joanna worried the sleeves of her worn pink hoodie. No matter the weather, rain or shine, the hoodie was a staple in her limited wardrobe. "Is he coming back to Cherish?"

"No." Scarlett shook her head as the familiar desolation crept in. All these years she'd dreamed of a man who would truly love her, a man who wanted to share her life.

How had she missed the most important part? She couldn't have a real relationship, because she was afraid to trust and had put up a protective shield.

With good reason. People always left, oftentimes without saying goodbye. She couldn't count on anyone except herself. In the end, she had probably pushed Judson away with her brash manner—an attempt to hide her insecurities.

"Dr. Troutman moved back to his family home in Arizona," she said. "His father fell ill, so he's helping his elderly mother. His parents also own a vet business, and he felt obligated to take it over. That's why he sold his practice here in Cherish."

There it was. More reasons why she had not only lost her fiancé, but also her job as his receptionist when the practice closed.

Quiet enveloped Scarlett and Joanna for a beat, broken by the chirping of a cherry-red cardinal frequenting a bird feeder, designed for the birds as well as the bird watchers.

Not far away, a forgotten Christmas ornament hung on a branch of a tall pine tree, the shiny silver bulb catching the sunlight.

Joanna reached for her dog-eared copy of *Fifteen* by Beverly Cleary. At ten years old, the girl was already an incurable romantic. "What about you? Dr. Troutman should've asked you to go with him."

Scarlett hung an arm around Joanna's thin shoulders. "He did. I refused."

He'd asked half-heartedly, but she didn't insert that part. Besides, she was too loyal to Joanna, her Little Sister, to leave her. For Joanna's sake, Scarlett needed to be dependable. The girl had experienced constant disappointment in her young life when her father had abandoned her and her family, and her childhood reminded Scarlett of her own unhappy past.

"Long ago," Scarlett said, "I made a decision to stay rooted in one spot for the rest of my life. I just didn't know where that spot was."

"So you decided on Cherish, South Carolina?" Joanna gave a horrified burst of laughter. "This town is way too small for me. I want to have an apartment in a big city when I'm eighteen."

"I lived in Chicago my entire childhood and tried to establish roots there as an adult. All I found were flashing neon signs, traffic lights at every corner, and car horns forever honking." Scarlett scooted closer to Joanna. "I landed here after I applied for the job as a receptionist for Dr. Troutman. And now I intend to stay because I love southern towns."

Certainly, people described Cherish as an *if you blink when you pass through, you'll miss it kind of place*, but the picturesque charm appealed to her. As soon as she'd arrived, she'd known she had finally found a hometown.

She reached into the pocket of her bright-yellow raincoat

and pulled out a slim chocolate candy bar. With a snap, she offered Joanna half, then glanced at her watch. "Hey, it's almost three o'clock. Wouldn't you rather hang out with your friends on the weekend than with me? It's not too late to text them."

"What friends?" The girl pushed out a dramatic sigh. "You know what I would give to have a real friend right now? Besides you, of course." With those wisely chosen last words, Joanna added an impish chuckle.

"Thanks," Scarlett joked sarcastically before her tone sobered. "Just remember I'm always here for you."

"I know." Pausing, Joanna took a breath. "Although it's just that … as usual, I'm the new girl in town."

"You came to Cherish in September, and it's January."

Before Scarlett could say more, Joanna frowned. Lately, she smiled often, so the frown was unexpected. "I'm uncomfortable when all the students in my class stare at me."

"Then stare back at them."

"I can't." The girl studied her hands. "I'm not friendly and loud like you."

Friendly was a good thing. Loud—not so good. Demure, polite, and ladylike were never traits Scarlett had mastered, but this was a new year. January, the season for fresh beginnings and resolutions.

Soothingly, she tucked a strand of Joanna's brown hair behind her ear. "Remember you're not the new girl anymore, although you're definitely the sweetest."

Scarlett had been matched with Joanna to be her mentor and Big Sister after she'd attended a recruitment asking for volunteers to give of their time. The Big Brothers Big Sisters program was community based, and it focused on low-income families.

Joanna's homelife consisted of her mother, Tania, a slight, ebony-haired woman who incessantly smoked; a scattering of younger siblings; and never enough money to get the family through the month.

"No, you're the sweetest," Joanna said, looking up at Scarlett. "And the prettiest. I wish I had red hair and green eyes and a gigantic smile."

Scarlett grinned, positioning herself so that she and Joanna could hold hands. Here in this park bordered by a hill, they could breathe in trees and fresh air and solitude. The past few months, the park bench had become their place to sit quietly together. Lately, the air smelled of spring—damp soil and grass and new birth.

God promised new beginnings in the normal trappings of daily life. He gave purpose to common situations. Surely, He would help Scarlett not only survive her heartbreak, but be strengthened by enjoying nature and this precious little girl.

Joanna eyed a clump of low-growing pansies, the deep-violet and eye-catching yellow adding vibrancy to the glistening green grass. "Not that I don't appreciate your candy, but I'd love for a boy to give me chocolate for Valentine's Day."

A boy? Stiffly, Scarlett drew back her head. Joanna was certainly growing up fast. She was only in fifth grade, although with today's social media and television programs, kids grew up faster than when Scarlett was young. Still, the idea was disconcerting. Shouldn't Joanna be more interested in roller skating or board games?

Still, she was tempted to say, *Me too*. She kept the contemplation to herself because a candy delivery wasn't coming her way anytime soon. She squeezed Joanna's hand. "But we have each other, right?"

"Right."

That morning had brought rain, a quick storm rattling trees and sweeping across tidy lawns in Scarlett's working-class neighborhood. Now the clouds had parted, and an afternoon sun emerged in a brilliant blue sky, a typical winter day in the Carolinas, where the weather changed from cold to warm within hours. Nearby, dogs barked and teenagers tossed Frisbees to each other.

Scarlett sat against the park bench while Joanna munched her chocolate bar.

"Aren't you going to eat your candy?" Joanna asked between mouthfuls.

"No. You can have mine too." Scarlett handed Joanna her half. She loved candy and crunchy peanut butter ice cream and all kinds of junk food, and deliberated for a half second before giving the candy bar up.

No, no, no. She pushed out a breath. She couldn't count the number of times she'd attempted to diet unsuccessfully. The lead balloon feeling of failure never left, nor its silent counterpart, shame.

Solid looking, people described her. Or, *She has such a pretty face.* Or her favorite, *She's big-boned.* All subtle reminders she should shed thirty pounds.

This time she would lose the weight, she vowed.

She'd heard the cabbage diet worked well, although she'd never liked cabbage.

Tomorrow. She'd begin a new diet tomorrow.

"C'mon, let's head back into town." Scarlett came to her feet and took Joanna's sticky hand in hers. "We can stop for a slice of pizza at Frank's Pizzeria."

At the end of the street, guitar music wafted toward them. People in the park reacted, drifting toward the music, bobbing their heads to the beat of a Christian contemporary song.

"'And we sing, you are our God ...'" The tenor male voice resonated through the air.

"Look, Scarlett." Joanna slowed and pointed to a poster mounted to a streetlamp. The poster advertised a Valentine-themed benefit concert sponsored by Musically Yours, the local music store and conservatory. The event would be held outdoors in the park, rain or shine.

The concert was being held to raise money for Cherish Elementary School's music program. Accompanying the poster was a picture of a good-looking man with dark wavy hair, stubble on his chin, and piercing blue eyes.

Joseph Slater, a Christian recording artist, was headlining the event.

"Isn't he handsome?" Joanna had eaten the entire candy bar, evidenced by smears of chocolate on her chin.

"Yes, but he's a musician," Scarlett said.

"Is that good?"

"It means he's busy recording and performing, so handsome doesn't count because he's unavailable." Scarlett read the poster listing his recent tours and managed a *wow*. Was he ever successful.

"A few months ago, I listened to one of his hits on the Christian station," Scarlett continued. "The DJ went on for five minutes about Joseph Slater because he writes all his own music, as well as songs for various Christian artists. And he was nominated for a Grammy award."

"I knew he was famous." Joanna tented her hands over her eyes and read aloud, "'An international recording phenomenon who recently returned from Australia and is touring the U.S.'" She had a breathless, excited look about her. "We should totally go to the show and meet him. Then you can fall in love again."

At the idea of it—love, dreaming new dreams—a shiver of longing quickened Scarlett's pulse. She believed in the possibility of happily ever after. Just not for her, and certainly not with a touring musician who was here today and gone tomorrow.

"They're selling tickets to the concert at Musically Yours."

Joanna tugged on Scarlett's hand. "Don't you know the people who own that music store?"

"Ryan and Dorothy Edwards are dear friends."

"Then you wouldn't want to disappoint your friends, right?"

The joy on Joanna's pale, freckled face had Scarlett fishing for her wallet and hoping she had enough money to cover the ticket prices.

"No disappointments allowed," she declared, counting out a wad of one-dollar bills.

"C'mon." Joanna was off like a rocket, her thin legs moving rapidly toward the music store.

Scarlett couldn't help her smile and quickened her pace. She wanted to attend the concert anyway because she appreciated all kinds of music.

As they rounded the corner, Joanna skidded to a stop. "That's him! I recognize his picture! Joseph Slater. Playing the guitar."

He sat on a stool in front of Musically Yours, his sharp profile outlined against a sunlit sky. In person, he was even more handsome than his photo. His wavy hair curled at the nape, framing a strong face, straight nose and chiseled jawline. Thoughtfully, he strummed his guitar and sang an inspirational melody to a small enchanted audience. They stood around him and listened intently.

He looked up after he sang his final number, the lyrics about love and peace particularly moving, the deep, rich timbre of his voice striking an unexpected chord in Scarlett's chest.

His clear blue eyes met her gaze.

She sucked in a breath, attempted to wave or applaud, but shelved the idea. Instead, she murmured, "I love that song," to no one in particular. For once, she'd really stopped and listened. The melody was beautiful, and the heartfelt lyrics about trusting God hit her emotionally.

Tears rose in her eyes and she brushed a hand across her lashes.

Silly. She was being silly. Usually, she didn't listen to Christian music, preferring top 40 hits. Besides, she didn't feel comfortable around men who were too good-looking, and this guy lifted drop-dead gorgeous to a whole new level. Attractive guys made her self-conscious about her weight. Besides, in her slick yellow raincoat, she probably resembled a chubby lemon.

She had no idea how many albums Joseph Slater had recorded, but made a mental note to Google him as soon as she returned to her apartment. He'd just topped the number-one spot on her hit list, edging out her favorite rock singer.

"He's staring at you," Joanna whispered.

No. Scarlett was staring at *him* like a gape-mouthed schoolgirl.

He set down his guitar, thanked the audience, and placed the guitar into its case. Smiling an acknowledgement to the cluster of fans, he shrugged on his worn leather jacket, picked up the case, and strode toward her.

Oh my. Now? She was coming face-to-face with him? Now? She must look the size of a house with her wrinkled cotton pants and red boots. And her sweater. She indulged in good cashmere sweaters, although this fitted charcoal-gray one sported a hot fudge sundae graphic on the front. Not exactly a motivation, but the idea of wearing a piece of celery made her inwardly chuckle.

A crisp breeze snapped through the air, and a loose strand of her curly hair fluttered across her forehead. The dampness of the earlier rain had caused her hair to frizz, and she probably looked like she'd been electrified.

As he approached, she felt a jolt of expectation. She and

Joanna exchanged glances, and Joanna gave a thumbs up. That is, until he angled past them with a polite smile and entered the music store.

*** End of Excerpt *A Valentine to Cherish* by Josie Riviera ***
Keep reading on Amazon. FREE on Kindle Unlimited.

ABOUT THE AUTHOR

Josie Riviera is a USA TODAY bestselling author of contemporary, inspirational, and historical sweet romances that read like Hallmark movies. She lives in the Charlotte, NC, area with her wonderfully supportive husband. They share their home with an adorable shih tzu, who constantly needs grooming, and live in an old house forever needing renovations.

Become a member of my Read and Review VIP Facebook group for exclusive giveaways and ARCs.

To connect with Josie, visit her webpage and subscribe to her newsletter. As a thank-you, she'll send you a free sweet romance novella delivered directly to your inbox.

http://josieriviera.com/

PRAISE AND AWARDS

USA TODAY bestselling author

#1 Amazon Bestseller Women's Religious Fiction
#1 Amazon Bestseller Contemporary Religious Fiction
#1 Amazon Bestseller Inspirational Religious Fiction
#2 Amazon Bestseller Inspirational Prayer

#1 Amazon Bestseller Religious Short Stories
#3 Amazon Bestseller Religious Romance
#21 Amazon Bestseller Holiday Fiction

5 STAR READER REVIEWS

"Cherish is a town you really want to visit! This boxed set brings you three separate stand alone stories to fall in love with. The characters may overlap, but the stories are true stand alone. Don't wait to read these! You will fall in love over and over again!"- Amazon Reviewer

"Josie Rivera has written this book with the sensitivity of the soul of a genuine musician who also has a deep understanding of God's love and His power of restoration in every area of life. She carefully crafts the personalities of her characters so that each one is unique, and the reader can easily identify with one or all of them. Her attention to detail is remarkable as she allows you to see people and places and to become a citizen of Cherish. You will want to stay there! Thanks Josie Riviera for enriching the Christmas season with this inspiring story." - Amazon Reviewer

"This was my first book of Josie Riviera's Cherish series that I had read/listen to and enjoyed her book very much. I have received the audible complementary to enjoy and this review is my honest thoughts on *A Christmas to Cherish.*

A Christmas to Cherish is about Emmanuelle Sumter who goes to Cherish in South Carolina to try to piece back her life and dreams after her life took a turn towards a dark path where she loses hope and trust in men. The other main character Deputy Nicholas Thompson who is struggling with his last relationship that left him hurt and numb. Years earlier Nicholas and Emmanuelle called/skype during a period where Nicholas sister and Emmanuelle best friend was in rehab, keeping each other strong and supporting each other emotionally during that time. But many years and things changed in both of their lives, but will they both get over their past or will their past catch up and entangle them in separate directions?" - Amazon Reviewer

ACKNOWLEDGMENTS

To my patient husband, Dave, and our three wonderful children.

ALSO BY JOSIE RIVIERA

Seeking Patience

Seeking Catherine (always Free!)

Seeking Fortune

Seeking Charity

Seeking Rachel

The Seeking Series

Oh Danny Boy

I Love You More

A Snowy White Christmas

A Portuguese Christmas

Holiday Hearts Book Bundle Volume One

Holiday Hearts Book Bundle Volume Two

Holiday Hearts Book Bundle Volume Three

Holiday Hearts Book Bundle Volume Four

Holiday Hearts Book Bundle Volume Five

Candleglow and Mistletoe

Maeve (Perfect Match)

A Love Song To Cherish

A Christmas To Cherish

A Valentine To Cherish

A Christmas Puppy To Cherish

A Homecoming To Cherish

A Summer To Cherish

Romance Stories To Cherish

Romance Stories To Cherish Volume Two

Cherished Hearts Six Book Volume

Aloha To Love

Sweet Peppermint Kisses

Valentine Hearts Boxed Set

1-800-CUPID

1-800-CHRISTMAS

1-800-IRELAND

1-800-SUMMER

1-800-NEW YEAR

The 1-800-Series Sweet Contemporary Romance Bundle

Irish Hearts Sweet Romance Bundle

Holly's Gift

A Chocolate-Box Christmas

A Chocolate-Box New Years

A Chocolate-Box Valentine

A Chocolate-Box Summer Breeze

A Chocolate-Box Christmas Wish

A Chocolate-Box Irish Wedding

Chocolate-Box Hearts

Chocolate-Box Hearts Volume Two

Chocolate-Box Double Hearts

Recipes From The Heart

Leading Hearts

New Year Hearts

SENIOR HEARTS

Summer Hearts

Christmas in the Air (1-800-Book)

A Very Christian Christmas

The 1-800-Series Volume Two

The 1-800-Series Complete

Christmas Tails of the Heart

Cocoa's Christmas Love

Pawfect Christmas Hearts

Pink Coral Island

Whispers of Love in Sweetwater Springs

Whispers of Maple Memories in Sweetwater Springs

Whispers of Holiday Magic in Sweetwater Springs

Whispers of Sweetwater Springs

A Harvest of Miracles

A Winter Promise

A Season Out of Time

Hearts and Horseshoes

Wishes and Wildflowers

1-800-CUPIDON (French Edition)

1-800-CUPIDO (Spanish Edition)

1-800-AMOR (German Edition)

Most books are available in ebook, audiobook, paperback, Large Print paperback and Hardcover.

Many are FREE on Kindle Unlimited!

A GIFT FOR YOU

To keep up on newly released ebooks, paperbacks, Large Print Paperbacks, audiobooks, as well as exclusive sales, sign up for Josie's Newsletter today.

As a thank you, I'll send you a Free PDF ... The Beauty Of ...

Josie's Newsletter

Did you know that according to a Yale University study, people who read books live longer?